A Note on the Author

Louise Couper was born in Dublin and graduated from Trinity College, Dublin. She now lives with her husband and two sons on an organic farm in Co Westmeath. She also runs her own business in Tullamore, Co Offaly and is a founder member of the Offaly Writers Group. *Philippa's Farm* is her first novel.

PHILIPPA'S FARM

PHILIPPA'S FARM

Louise Couper

POOLBEG

Published in 1995 by
Poolbeg Press Ltd,
Knocksedan House,
123 Baldoyle Industrial Estate,
Dublin 13, Ireland

A catalogue record for this book is available from the British Library.

ISBN 1 85371 217 5

Cover painting *Evening Mist* by Stephen Darbishire
By courtesy of Richard Hagen Ltd,
Yew Tree House, Broadway, Worcestershire
Cover design by Poolbeg Group Services Ltd
Set by Poolbeg Group Services Ltd in Goudy
Printed by The Guernsey Press Ltd,
Vale, Guernsey, Channel Islands.

For David

"I was always dying to meet you; I thought you looked such a happy person."

"That's very nice of you, Emily," I replied, silently congratulating myself on creating the right impression. The reality couldn't be further from the truth but nobody likes a sourpuss.

"I've always wondered how you do it, Philippa, is it yoga, or maybe acupuncture, or perhaps you've read that book that's all the rage, some Indian doctor wrote it. All to do with auras and ionisers."

Emily continued to list the What's What on guides to becoming wonderful as we wove our way through Ballinamore and at last headed for the Slieve Blooms.

"No, I haven't come across any of those," I said. I felt like adding that it was the Book of Life that taught me whatever I know but bit my tongue. Emily after all was not a friend, merely a member, like myself, of the Esker Archaeological Society.

"Well," she said, folding her arms and slumping even further into the seat of the car, "I've read every book under the sun from *Your Life can be made Whole* to *How to Roll Away that Spare Tyre* and I'm none the wiser."

I could identify with the denouement but I didn't want to create the cosy atmosphere of "you tell me some of your little trials and tribulations and I'll tell you some of mine" so beloved of female twosomes. Instead, I concentrated on spotting the road to Clareen where we hoped to find Saighir Kieran, an early Christian monastic settlement lying abandoned at the side of the mountains, forgotten, except that is, for the dedicated few who pored over its ruins when the weather was fine.

The rest of the group had gone ahead. We got delayed with Emily's period arriving as we were about to leave. She rushed off for the bathroom as Dickie, her husband, came towards me.

"Come and wait inside," Dickie said. At seven in the evening still clad in his pinstripe.

"I hear you're a gardener," he said. "Care to see my marrows?" He looked at me hopefully. How could I refuse? I took one of the children with me, just in case.

We bumbled our way into the polytunnel. It was airless and damp like the banana house in the Botanic Gardens. Giant marrows sported their pendulous bosom shapes atop the most reeking of dung heaps.

"How interesting," was all I could manage between trying to breathe and stopping the child from lifting my skirt.

"It's fascinating," Dickie added with emphasis. "And this," he said, patting an enormous black container, "is the secret of success. My recipe. It's all in the preparation of the sustenance: the purest of cane sugar, honey, propolis extract for antibiotics and the cleanest of spring water. And of course, love is important. They adore the human voice and touch," he said, caressing the largest of the marrows like a farmer feeling a cow's udder.

Just as I began to feel very hot and dizzy, Emily reappeared. I made my apologies and beat a hasty retreat, regretting my foolhardiness in leaving my cosy little farm. It was years since I had forsaken the noise and smell of the city and its population for the peace and fresh air of the countryside. But one must venture into the world now and again if only to realise how fortunate one is.

Emily took out her specs and studied the map. The road is a long, narrow ribbon from Ballinamore and then turns right to skirt the mountain. We passed tiny Adamstown. A group of children were earthing up potato ridges on the steep bank of the Silver River. An old man was sawing logs, while on the hill behind him another was digging the garden.

"We go through Kinnitty," Emily said, "and then on to Clareen. Then somewhere to the left is the monastery. I believe the old church has a very good Sheela-na-Gig."

"Oh good!" I said sincerely. "The witch on the wall."

I was glad to hear there would be something to see. I had joined the Archaeological Society for much the same reason that I prefer to be a driver than a passenger. There was an object always to hand when things got a bit awkward. The decoration of a Romanesque capital or the careless drivers on the road are so useful when things take a dangerous turn and get too near the bone. I'll never forget the time when, in the middle of the Long Room in Trinity College, as Professor Maximilian O'Connor waxed lyrical about the intricacies of the Book of Kells, Gaye Greene informed me and, *par hasard*, most of the people present, how she never in her life "got any pleasure from sex with Percy", her husband. I was torn with curiosity to know whether she ever got any pleasure from sex at all or who it was she had enjoyed it with. However, I restrained myself and the Book came to my rescue.

"Exquisite lattice work and configuration," I whispered as loudly as I dared without drowning out the Professor. "Look at the cheeky little fellow at the top of the page." It did the trick and she quietened down.

We were through Kinnitty and took the left turn for Roscrea. Emily seemed to have switched off.

At Clareen she came to life and past the crossroads she squealed, "There they are!" as the rest of the group came into view.

There were waves and hellos everywhere. I didn't bother; I often feel women could be more economical with their energy.

Emily bounced onto the grass and greeted the others like long-lost friends. There was much talk about the inaccessibility of the ruins, about the new fence which appeared to be electrified, effectively cutting us off from the monastery unless we were willing to clamber over the wall. Though still shapely and having just had a wax job, I didn't particularly relish exposing my thighs to all and sundry. In the end, good old Noreen Mulready, ever practical, came to our rescue. From the boot of her car she produced two sun chairs.

"Well girls, if we put one on either side of the wall, we'll have a class of a stile. How's that for lateral thinking?" Of course, I bit my tongue.

"You're a genius," Emily smiled, offering to be the first to clamber over. I went next and found once I heaved my bottom onto the wall I could use it as a pivot to swing my legs. Quite painless, really.

The tiny, ruined monastery lay scattered before us, a jigsaw of rocks and stones and ivy. We fanned out, pink and white cardigans, like blobs of marshmallow. Except for me; I merged with the greeny-yellow grass and grey stones in my tweeds and cashmere.

"Now!" boomed Noreen, "who's the expert on this era?"

"I haven't a clue about anything prior to the eighteenth century," Clara shouted back. She really hadn't a clue about anything, except the few facts they teach you in nursing school.

We stood still, arms folded, staring at the rubble. I enjoy these moments of tension, the eye flickers of unease, the tell-tale shifting of feet. I can be most nearly myself then, when the others are preoccupied.

I left them to it and sorted through the stones, tracing the lines of tiny buildings. How so many people managed to live in such a small area amazed me. Perhaps people were smaller then, neater trim, without our avoirdupois?

Little pink cranesbill flourished in the gaps and cracks. Were they there all those years ago? The church itself stood a little apart, its walls still standing. In the cool of its shadow clouds of midges hopped in the air. I pulled my blouse tighter around my neck and regretted not dousing myself with *Jungle Formula*.

Quite suddenly I saw it, high up, staring out across the valley. The others were behind me now.

"Philippa, you sly old thing, going ahead of us," someone said. I didn't bother replying. I pointed to my touchstone, my find.

As one, heads were thrown back, gazing up at the image. A face with staring eyes and skeletal chest sat with legs bent, exposing her all.

"My God Almighty," Emily gasped in horror, staring at the stone.

"Thank God none of the men are here," Gaye Greene, the inorgasmic one, stated with relief.

"I wonder is that position physically possible?" asked Clara, consulting her internal *Gray's Anatomy*.

"It looks painful anyway," Noreen replied. "But they say you get used to anything. Sure look at them Yogis lying on beds of nails with not a bother on them."

"You sound almost eager to learn, Noreen," I smiled.

"Well now, Philippa," she replied, good sport that she is, "I'll ask the library to get me a copy of the *Kama*whateveritis and I'll let you know how me and Seamus get on!"

I heard the sting in her reply, a reference to my spinsterhood.

A silence fell. We continued to stare at the figure, though at this stage my neck was aching.

"Well, more power to her elbow, or whatever it is," Noreen smiled. "If she can bend her legs like that, expose herself without shame, isn't it completely natural and God made us the way he meant us to be, so what's sauce for the goose is sauce for the gander."

"I'm sure there's blasphemy there somewhere, Noreen," Emily said, smoothing an invisible crease in her jumper. "Our Lord never indulged in matters of the flesh when he was on this earth, so we can't really say it's what we were made for."

"Doesn't everything reproduce itself and what is it all for but that? So I say it's all natural," said Noreen.

I was riveted at this stage and decided to add fuel to the fire.

"I think what Emily is trying to say is that reproduction is all right, provided you take no pleasure in it."

"So, what's the answer, artificial insemination?" Noreen asked. "I suppose that's what the Immaculate Conception was after all."

We pondered on that for an instant. I didn't dare reply.

The picnic came to our rescue. We always bring one as our jaunts often take us off the beaten track where the kind of coffee shop we like is as alien as pitta bread and herbal tea on the Aran Islands.

Clara makes wonderful chocolate cake and Gaye Greene invariably brings dull but freshly made sandwiches. I bring the cutlery and china tea-set, which means I don't have any leftovers to gnaw my way through for the rest of the week. I also think tea tastes so much better from a china cup.

The little picnic table was erected in seconds. Clara tossed on the red gingham cover. "Just because you're away from civilised living there's no reason to behave like a savage," my mother always said. So we always observe the niceties. I even put a few cranesbill in a mustard pot to decorate the table.

Clara and I are the water-bearers, so we took off for the little stream at the bottom of the hill.

Clara is a great one for hygiene and washed out the pot thoroughly. Her training as a nurse leaks into her life; all is antiseptic. She trusts me to have the cups and cutlery practically sterile.

"That was a bit ikey up there with your woman on the church," Clara leaned conspiratorially towards me. "I was glad it finished when it did. It could have got very odd. Maybe women shouldn't really go out on their own, without men. They need a restraining influence on them."

"That's precisely why I never succumbed to the matrimonial state, Clara," I confided. "I'd rather be me, warts and all, than an appendage, forever pleasing, forever dull."

"Oh, I'd give anything to be married. To have my own kitchen spick and span; jars of spices and herbs ranged along the wall, stacks of newly washed tea towels in drawers, blinding white nappies on the line and a freshly-washed baby gurgling happily in its pram."

"Well, Clara, I wish you well. I'd love to think it would be as simple as that but there's the inescapable fact of 'the other', freshly cleaned tea towels used to wipe engine parts, baby puking up its dinner all over its clean clothes. There's the contamination factor, like the traces of iron in the water which in time turns the nappies yellow."

I perhaps showed more feeling that I would have wished. Clara looked at me as she does sometimes when she's thinking what an oddball I am. I could have put her mind at rest and told her my life story, its joys and losses but I feared her clinical analysis, her attempt to disinfect my unacceptable parts.

When we got back to put the kettle on the gas, there was a silence except for the gentle sobbing of Gaye Greene.

Clara, ever helpful, ever intrusive, ran to her side, offering her one of the soft white napkins I had brought. Extremely irritating. We only had four.

"Do you want to talk about it, Gaye?" Noreen demanded.

I wanted to tell her to mind her own business, but I busied myself with the tea things instead.

"Well, I was fine, fine," she answered, blowing her nose on the napkin. "It was just seeing that figure person, on top of the wall. It affected me. It reminded me so much of myself."

Gaye Greene hanging out of the church gable, *déshabillé*, quite a sight!

"How was that like yourself, Gaye?" Noreen went on relentlessly.

"Well, she's telling the world, here I am, come and have me. I'm yours. But it doesn't seem to do any good. She seems to be just stuck at that, not getting anywhere."

"And where would she like to get?"

"Well, she'd like not to have to do that all the time. She'd like to feel she had what she wanted for the time being. I suppose," she said quietly, "I suppose she'd like to feel fulfilled."

I felt like an eavesdropper on something very private. I thought we should move away, leave Gaye in peace. But something held me. I looked at Noreen and saw a tear sitting on top of the plump roundness of her cheek and then at Emily, who was biting her lip. I thought of Dickie, lavishing all that care and love on his family of marrows. A cloud of sadness enveloped me. I thought again of the "Witch on the Wall" and I thought about myself, self-sufficient and quietly cosy, though loveless and childless. Had I frightened off all suitors with my desire? Had I been too honest in my longing? Perhaps I should have hidden it, pretended nonchalance, lack of ardour, frigidity even.

I handed Gaye Greene a cup of tea, took the soggy napkin from her and gave her mine.

"Perhaps it's not too late, Mrs Greene," I suggested, my voice crackling. The thought brought a little sparkle to her eyes.

I busied myself with the china and cutlery, while Clara squeezed the last drop of brown from the tea-bags.

The evening deteriorated rapidly and as I folded the table cloth and stowed everything away for the next outing, I resolved that no matter who asked me what our meetings were like I would tell them they were always madly, madly gay. It just wouldn't do to give the right impression.

"Maybe we ought to invite the men to come the next time. Give us a different perspective. We can't be always indulging ourselves," Noreen declared, putting the last of the picnic things into the boot.

I couldn't see why not, though Clara would be pleased. The next best thing to a single man was one who was unhappily hitched. There seemed to be one or two of those around.

Having wished Emily good-night and foregoing her supper invitation, I stopped by McGahern's pub for a well-deserved nightcap.

"How's it going?" I asked the old man as he put the whiskey into a bag with a shaky hand.

"Sure one foot in front of the other," he said, slapping the change on the counter.

God is merciful. Old man McGahern is one of the few bachelors in Ballinamore. Perhaps I ought to let Clara know.

"We'll need to bring a little flask of something," Emily said on the phone. "You know what men are like."

Indeed I do but I said nothing. The men had accepted the invitation to come on our next outing. I'd felt like not going and then changed my mind. There's no point in giving in to that sort of pressure. Men have it every way.

It was to be a long trip this time, seeing the ladies wouldn't have to rush back to get supper. Lough Gur in County Limerick was chosen. Lunch would be *en route*, since the men would be paying, and the customary picnic was reserved for the return journey. A professor from the University of Limerick was even laid on to fill our minds with the correct facts. Nothing was to be left to chance.

Although in the throes of cheese-making and with several gallons of elderflower champagne bubbling away, I decided I could do with a break. However, I loaded the picnic basket with a heavy heart. It had seemed like sacrilege to allow any of the men to drink from one of my china cups. Delph mugs would be more appropriate. Then, as I often do, I relented and said to hell with it, perhaps they could do with a bit of civilising.

Of course after that, I warmed to the task and put in my good silver apostle teaspoons, a gift from a prospective mother-in-law just before I discovered the truth about her son. I never gave them back and she was too ashamed to ask for them. I don't feel the least bit guilty.

"Who is going in your car?" Emily Delaney asked. It's always Emily who phones, never Noreen or Gaye Greene. I sometimes wonder why.

"I don't mind who comes with me. Whoever needs a lift, I suppose. Except, if you don't mind, I'd rather not have Gaye and Percy Greene. His legs are too long."

So I locked up the chickens and ducks, gave Nanny a good feed of flaked maize and rolled barley and tucked the picnic basket under my arm.

We met in the Square in Ballinamore. I didn't feel my usual ebullient self as I parked the car and finished my bar of chocolate. Ah well, onward, ever onward, as usual. Happiness has to be worked at. Joy is something else.

I marched boldly up to them and gave my best smile. Emily's Dickie had on his pinstripe. He seems to have been born in the thing. His primrose shirt matched the whites of his eyes. I always think of marrows when I look at him. Large and soft.

Gaye Greene looked like a little girl out with Daddy. Her Laura Ashley gear, straw hat, white dress with blue yachts sailing on red seas reminded me of my "Mary Mary Quite Contrary" sampler, though her hiking boots were decidedly out of place.

Percy Greene was expending a lot of energy trying to look as if he couldn't care less. His long legs were clad in rich plum and finished in white socks and tiny shoes with tassels and a gold chain across the upper. A pink handkerchief was artistically arranged in the top pocket of a waistcoat of very fine calfskin. The matching pink shirt highlighted the acne craters on his face. He and Dickie Delaney seemed to be getting on like long-lost friends, Dickie making what looked like marrow shapes in the air and Percy puckering his lips in an "ooo" as if he was about to kiss someone. I felt I'd already had enough.

"Well, girl, ye recovered, I see," Noreen said, her breast brushing my arm, "from the Slieve Blooms," she pressed.

"Of course! A wonderful evening; absolutely amazing place."

"It didn't give you any bad thoughts?"

"None that I didn't have already, Noreen." It slipped

out a trifle too archly. However, I can't be always watching myself.

"I'd say you've many a tale to tell. You're not as green as yer cabbage is painted, I'd say."

I looked at the shrimp of a man beside her.

"This is Seamus. And this," she said grabbing his sleeve, "is the famous Philippa."

The "famous" startled me a bit. I put out my hand to receive a bundle of tiny, bony fingers with a decided shake. I hoped he wouldn't take any risk with my good china. I resolved to keep an eye on him. Perhaps the mugs would have been a good idea after all.

"Not so fast," Emily yelled as we were about to escape to our various cars. "Just line up against the war memorial."

She took out her instamatic and pointed it at the motley crew. Percy and Gaye smiling like lunatics, Seamus and Noreen Mulready glued together, though not happy about it. I looked at Dickie and said to Emily, "You take your rightful place with your nearest and dearest, I'll do the honours."

I'd no wish to have a record of my foolhardiness. Teresa and Dotty, our newest recruits, brought up the rear with their happy holiday grins and I clicked just as Emily pushed her hand through Dickie's arm.

We dispersed quietly. Noreen had decided who was going with whom. She had already booked her seat in Percy's Merc. When I opened the door of my humbler conveyance, there was Seamus at my heels, assumption written all over his face. I didn't want to make a fuss, so I said nothing. I decided he would sit in the front, where he could be watched.

Teresa and Dotty were still standing round. I saw my chance.

"Come on girls, plenty of room here," I shouted and bundled them into the back seat.

"Thank you so much, Miss Woodcock," they chorused like two robins perched on a branch. Whatever hope I had fleetingly entertained of drowning out Seamus had now evaporated.

"Unusual name – Woodcock," Seamus said, as I started the engine.

Here we go, I thought.

"I won't mention pheasants or partridge. I'm sure you've heard everything in your time."

"Everything," I replied, my foot a little too heavily on the accelerator. I didn't seem to have my usual grip on myself.

"Funny things, names," he went on. "There's a fella over by Rosenallis by the name of Mick Rabbitt who married a Josie Bunny. At the time things were said about hoppin' into burrows and mixintheirtoeses and breedin' like you know whats. I suppose," he said, staring pointedly at me, "a certain class of person could take it up in a serious kind of way but it was all harmless enough."

I finally decided Seamus Mulready was a vulgar little man and Noreen had all my sympathy. I busied myself with the road. He turned to see how he was affecting the rear passengers. I could have sworn he winked. I pressed the accelerator even harder and gritted my teeth.

"Oh, I just love little bunnies," Dotty lisped, "all thoft and cuddly."

"So charming with their big ears and little tails."

"A bit like yourself," Seamus said, sniggering in the way men do when they think they've made a wonderful joke that will shock teacher. I pretended to sneeze.

We had booked lunch at Matt the Thresher's in Birdhill on my suggestion. They serve the best mussels in garlic butter I've ever tasted.

Once away from the car, I made a beeline for more civilised company. Even Gaye Greene seemed desirable.

"You've deserted your lord and master," I said as I caught up with her.

"I'm so fed up with Percy and his train set and Dickie and his marrows. They've talked about nothing else all morning," she complained.

"Well, let's you and me have a nice little chat. I know just the spot," I said, leading her towards my favourite nook. The table was full of empty dishes but we soon put it to rights.

"I think, Mrs Greene, we deserve a little treat," I said as I ordered two large gins. It was a lifesaver and went down in next to no time.

"I feel human now," Gaye Greene giggled dangerously. This worried me. I hoped she wouldn't let the side down. I felt on top of my form but I pretended to be just the same as usual.

The mussels arrived, swimming in garlic butter. We picked them from their shells and mopped up the warm butter with brown bread.

"How's it going with Seamus?" Mrs Greene asked, relaxing after her second gin and half the mussels. "I hope he's behaving himself, although I dare say you would be well able for him, Philippa."

"Physically certainly. A mind like a sewer," I answered, raising my head from a clean plate. Why do they never serve enough of the things?

"Of course," I pointed out, "it's all just to shock. Inside every man there's a small boy trying to get the better of mummy. It's best not to react. That only gives them satisfaction and encouragement. I'm afraid I slipped up rather badly there."

"I wonder what he's like at home. Is he, you know, very demanding on Noreen?"

"People are seldom what they seem, though the vision of mating they conjure up leaves me speechless."

We sucked at the shells in silence.

I felt almost glad to be alive as we climbed back into the car an hour later. Seamus and his shenanigans were as nothing. I even got a bit of a sing-song going and we entered the watery domain of Lough Gur with *I Love to go A-Wandering*.

We were the first to arrive. I put on my walking shoes and covered myself with *Jungle Formula* to ward off the midges and horse flies. Seamus begged for some and I willingly obliged, patting a generous amount on his spotty neck. How it must have stung, poor thing, but he didn't bat an eyelid.

"Not even Noreen will go near you now, Seamus," I said, jocularly.

"Fat chance of that anyway," he said with a bit too much feeling for my taste. Men should learn to keep their problems to themselves. Women have enough to cope with.

We turned towards the mock prehistoric hut. A familiar shape stood outside. Surely not, I thought, my heart thumping like mad. He looked towards us. Edward Henderson. I should have had my hair done and worn my new tartan jacket. Perhaps he wouldn't know me. After all, it was years and years ago.

"Pippy," he shrieked at me. I could have killed him. The others would lap it all up. I gave him one of my looks and he quietened down.

Of course, Seamus was close on my heels, affability personified.

"Grand spot here," he said to Eddie. "Knew what they were doing when they struck camp hereabouts. A power of reasoning for savages." Trust Seamus. Fools rush in. Dotty and Teresa simpered at his wonderful insight.

"You must be the Perfessor. Seamus Mulready at your service, Sir."

"Edward Henderson," Eddie replied nonplussed. I tried

15

to recover, to breathe again. I gave my hair a surreptitious fluff-up. He was still good-looking. The beard added an air of distinction. I always liked the wide-mouthed smile. Particularly the mouth.

A rather unruly mob we made when we had all assembled. I scarcely heard a word Edward said. I regretted the gin. It made me giddier than I cared to admit to.

We ambled into the largest of the huts. Edward put on the video. The ladies were on benches at the top. The men kept to the rear. I stood in the shadows at the back. As I had hoped, Eddie was soon beside me.

"Honestly Pippy, I can hardly believe it. You haven't changed at all. 'The beauty with the brains' we used to call you. Still that disturbing stare. Is the tongue as sharp?"

"Unfortunately, Eddie, I've had to learn moderation. It's taken most of the fun out of life, I'm afraid."

"Don't compromise, Pippy. You end up like me, a dusty old professor in a dusty old history department, yellowing like the pages of a manuscript."

I thought of my little farm, all neatly laid out in paddocks, its little pond and its woodland and inside, the dolls houses and teddy bears. All silent, speechless. Is it what I wished for all those years ago when Eddie and I argued whether life imitated art or the other way round and finished up in bed with a bottle of burgundy and a soul full of passion?

Out of the corner of my eye I spotted Dickie Delaney and Percy Greene merge with the timbers, very close together. Mr Greene was stroking the back of Dickie's head, following its shape to the nape of his neck. I thought about marrows and shoes with tassels, marriage and compromise.

Seamus sneaked towards Emily and spirited away the picnic basket. The rest of the men followed him outside while Noreen, Emily, Dotty and Teresa gazed at the screen, absorbed in the images of the past, altogether safer, more romantic than the present. I felt I needed some air.

Seamus and his cronies were seated at the picnic table, clouds of smoke billowing and Emily's flask glinting in the sun as it was passed around.

"If it isn't Pippy, me old golden delicious," Seamus announced, wiping his mouth on his sleeve. "'The beauty with the brains', they used to call her." An eavesdropper too.

If only I'd used them. Would I be here if I had?

A cold gust of wind came up from the lake. I buttoned my cardigan and walked past.

"A bad idea, bringing the men," Emily said, joining me beside the water's edge.

I wasn't sure whether it was a question or a statement. I continued to throw stones and watch them make ripples, spreading wider and wider. If only we could be as effective, make such a mark.

"Now that they've seen what we're up to, perhaps they'll no longer be interested."

"I'm afraid it's the opposite, Philippa. They think the whole thing is gas. Another excuse for a drink. As if they didn't have enough of them. Why do they always have to muscle in on everything just when it's going well? A pity Clara didn't come, she'd have fixed them."

"Too busy, I presume."

"Yes, working nights at the hospital. Not like her to miss an outing."

Especially with men around. Wait until she hears about Eddie.

"I think I need a holiday, Emily. I've worked very hard recently. What with Nanny having twins and having to feed the little lamb that was rejected by its mother, I need a rest."

17

"Just what I was saying to Noreen. She said you were too obsessed with your farm to leave it but I said to her you always knew when enough was enough."

How well Emily understood something about me. Perhaps she'd like an extra duckling at Christmas.

Emily agreed to look after everything while I was away. At this time of year, the little farm almost ran itself. It was neat and compact. The house was old and the back was enclosed by a yard with single storey buildings. Beyond these was an orchard with apples, greengages and plums. The sheep were there at the moment, eating the windfalls which were always too bruised to store well.

The barn stood to the left of the orchard, newer and taller, full of sweet green hay to feed the animals in winter. At the side of the house I had made my garden and protected it from hungry tummies by a dry-stone wall. Its deep black soil was fed with compost and seaweed meal. In winter, to cover the soil and avoid leaching of nutrients, I planted rye. In spring, I dug it in to provide the soil with its lifeblood, organic matter. Without this there would be no worms and without worms the soil would be dead, unable to feed any plants.

The autumn rains had begun, so the vegetables would bulk up to be harvested on my return. However, Emily had misgivings.

"But Aran, Philippa," Emily said, concern dripping down the phone line, "not a bit dull for you?"

"Where I'm at, just this moment, Emily, dullness has its compensations."

Besides, Aran was far from dull. At eighteen, I found it the most exciting place on earth. Largely due to the

19

presence of a certain six foot tall, blond Norwegian. We caused a little stir by borrowing a curragh and disappearing into the Atlantic for a few hours. I hoped the islanders had forgotten all about me and the incident hadn't been inscribed in the annals.

Emily said September is a dreadful time to go away, all the children would be back at school and their parents at the sink and desk respectively. Exactly. I could count on a little privacy and no members of the Archaeological Society.

"Why not the Canaries?" Emily further questioned.

Endless sun, chips and topless women disporting themselves before leering men was not my idea of fun.

"The Canaries wouldn't appeal to me, Emily. I really want somewhere quiet, somewhere I can get away from it all."

Going abroad held no guarantees, as I discovered the year I went to Nice. The second day who should I run into sipping wine in the Place Rossetti but the last man who saw me with my clothes off. Of course, it worked out well and we spent a very pleasant *soirée*, drinking Provence's splendid Rosé and dining on *bouillabaisse*. Dr Garland is a charming gynae-man, especially without his white coat and plastic gloves, and his wife was particularly intriguing. After a few glasses of wine, she waxed lyrical about the benefits to be had from mustard poultices.

However, not all such holiday encounters end as happily.

I took the ferry from Rossaveal to Kilronan. The water was choppy from a stiff breeze but I was quite snug in my blue wax jacket and woollen cap. One of the nice things about holidays is that you can travel incognito, in mufti. I bring with me all my shredded, though comfortable, jumpers. I can't bear to throw anything out. I bring something decent for the evenings. You never know.

The cold spray lashed between the boat and the pier as I tried to get off. It bit into my face and sat there like petrified tears. Not the sort of place to unload Gucci suitcases.

Kearney's Bed & Breakfast was at the harbour, a pink, two-storey house with the remnants of summer's flowers in boxes on the windows.

"We thought you wouldn't make it this day," a stout, red-faced and friendly woman, presumably the "Mrs Sean Kearney" of the brochure, gushed at the door. "There's a storm brewing and they don't like taking the boats out, even though it's money lost, a few pints the less that night. But here ye are, safe and sound, thanks be," she said as she took my bag and swirled her great tweed skirt towards the stairs.

"You'll have the best room in the place. Where I spent me honeymoon," she said with a titter. "Is it Mrs or Miss? I couldn't make it out on the phone."

"Just call me Philippa. No need to stand on ceremony," I said as lightly as I could but of course sounding as pompous as bedamned. After a few gins I might tell her a bit more.

"I'll bring a cup of tea and a ham sangwich in a while. You relax now, get your strength back. There's a bit of a sing-song in Dillon's pub if you've a mind for a bit of company later. Visitors are few on the ground this time of year. But there's a nice man in the room next to you. From England. A writer," she emphasised, as if that sealed his credentials.

To be avoided at all costs.

"I'll see how I'm fixed," was all the commitment I gave.

The room was large. Pine floorboards with sheepskin rugs. An old washstand stood to attention in a corner, its jug empty. The linen towel hanging from the rail smelled fresh. The pillows were frilled with lace, handmade with cotton

21

thread. Probably blinded the maker. I was pleased to see the bedcover and curtains bore no relation to each other: the bed was blue and the curtains bright yellow. The modern penchant for matching everything is so boring. It was beside the window with a view out to sea. The other tiny window looked out onto a back garden with a few rows of potatoes, their haulms yellow and sprawling, their energy spent. I lay on the bed, staring at the water. This was what I came for. An uninterrupted view, no telephone and no callers.

When I awoke it was pitch black and very cold. A plate of sandwiches covered in clingfilm was on the bedside table. The teapot was cold. I devoured the sandwiches, swilling them down with a few mouthfuls of *Maçon Villages* which I had brought, just in case. Within minutes I felt human again. It might even be fun to investigate this sing-song in the pub.

I donned my best holiday plumes – green boots and matching moleskin trousers with a hand-knitted jumper, stitched with mountains and cottages. I tied my hair back in a green velvet ribbon. Not bad for my age, I thought as I looked in the mirror. Not a day over ninety.

The pub was at the top of the village, a steep climb along a narrow road, about a donkey cart in width. A lungful of the salty, turf-smoke air almost sent me reeling; shallow breathing would be safer. The music from Dillon's got louder and louder. Maybe I should give it a miss, get an early bed. To hell with it, I was on holiday.

The room swirled with cigarette smoke and stank of spilt stout. Mrs Kearney came from the edge of the bar to greet me.

"You were sleeping like a babby. I didn't think you'd budge. Come and have something to warm you up."

She brought me to the bar where Sean Kearney, her nearest and dearest, his face shining, grabbed both my hands.

"Good girl now," he shouted, "you can give us a bar of a song later."

Over my dead body.

"Get that into you now, girl," he said, handing me a steaming whiskey alive with black cloves. "It'll banish the rawness of the night," he added, squeezing my leg. I smiled as sincerely as I could and took a grateful swig.

"I was just saying to Mr Kearney how you put me in mind of a young girl who stayed hereabouts, oh, it must be near on fifteen year ago. You've got the look of her. A bit unsteady she was, fell in with bad company."

"How unfortunate," I mumbled, chewing a clove.

"The men spent the day lamenting the loss of the curragh and the women feared for the child's safety."

How wicked I was. Enjoying every minute of it. Not so much losing my virginity as discovering what a waste of time it was. Keeping it for whom?

"Well, don't worry, Mrs Kearney, she probably got her comeuppance."

I felt Mr Kearney's ears flap a bit.

"Wonderful atmosphere," I said quickly.

"Sure it's the best place on earth," he said lifting the glass of black liquid and swallowing the lot. "The next parish to America," he said, dismissing the white froth on his mouth with the back of his hand.

He winked at the barman. Another glass of stout appeared. Mrs Sean disappeared into the Ladies.

I turned towards the barman to pay for the stout and the second hot whiskey which appeared.

"Allow me," a voice behind me said, putting a £20 note onto the counter.

I turned to see someone tall, elegantly greying at the temples. Definitely male. His blue tweed jacket had bright red flecks.

"Well Sean, have you introduced them yet?" Mrs

Kearney, smelling of Palmolive and slightly breathless, asked on her return.

"This is Gerald Ransome," she said, and added behind her hand to me, "he's in the room next to you." The famous writer. I decided to be on my guard. Writers tend to toss up the previous day's encounters into tomorrow's salad of boring stories. I refuse to be anyone's copy. I shook his offered hand, only just firmly enough.

"Philippa Woodcock."

He said he was delighted – but charm is the stock-in-trade of the Englishman, so I took that with a pinch of salt. Nevertheless, he did buy me another drink.

Sean Kearney seemed to find something hilariously amusing and was busy spluttering his pint all over the place. Mrs Kearney gave him a sharp kick to no avail and looked at me, flushed with embarrassment.

"Don't mind him, Philippa. You've a gorgeous name."

I might have guessed. Another Seamus. They seem to be everywhere.

"You're probably very uncomfortable here, Philippa," said Mrs Kearney, giving her husband daggers looks. "Let me see if there's a seat. Yes, down there by the side of Fiacra Óg O'Donnell. Maybe, Mr Ransome, you'd escort Philippa here down to it. On ye go now, we'll come after."

A likely story. Like two small children sent to the back of the classroom, Gerald and I crept down the side of the lounge and found the table. I cursed Mrs Kearney and her clumsy match-making, though he seemed okay except for those worrying flecks of red in the blue tweed bursting here and there in passionate eruptions.

"I suppose you're here to probe the native psyche," I said because I couldn't stand the tension. He took out a Biro and stirred his Martini and soda with it. No standing on ceremony.

"Holiday, actually, but people interest me too." I felt

uneasy, wondering where to go from here. So I did the next best thing and had a sip myself. I would make this one last the evening. Too much whiskey on top of wine would not be sensible.

I'd like to have asked why he was on holiday alone, where was Mrs Ransome. The man read my mind.

"I usually take a holiday in September when the last chapter has been sent to the publishers. This is my second visit here. Very different to London. I enjoy the sea."

I'd like to have agreed with him but I felt he might think I was saying what a lot in common we have, so I nodded instead. I still wondered about Mrs Ransome.

"And you, may I call you Philippa? What brings you here?" he asked, his eyes fixed on mine, his head slightly inclined.

The charm was so seductive I felt like blathering away. But I held back, wondered what was behind it. I think that's the attraction of archaeology, it fulfils a need to know what's beneath the surface, to discover to what the landscape owes its little bumps and hollows. I merely said, "A holiday away from it all. Time to think."

"You think that's a good thing?"

He shifted a leg and turned towards me, smiling.

I ignored the question and asked, "And how is Mrs Ransome?" I just couldn't resist it.

"Probably bone at this stage. Very dead anyway. Very dead." He swallowed the last of his Martini.

I decided then and there I wasn't going to feel the least bit guilty for asking. It wasn't my fault his wife was dead. And I wasn't going to mouth the usual platitudes. I never knew the woman, after all, and I'd only just met the widower.

The band became a timely distraction. There were two accordions and a fiddle creating quite a noise. The microphone seemed to be up for grabs. Sean Kearney was lurching towards it.

The meaning of the song was lost on me, I'm afraid. It was in the most arcane Irish I had heard. Although once upon a time an Irish scholar, the language meant little more than something cute to use when away in foreign parts where no one knew the intricacies of the Tuisheal Guineadach.

Rapturous applause greeted the end of the song, which of course encouraged further effort.

"And now, in honour of a guest here among us on our little island, I'd like to dedicate the next little number to Philippa – there she is, Ladies and Gentlemen."

I could have murdered him. I looked at Gerald for a little moral support in the teeth of this outrage but all he could do was smile and clap.

"Philippa Wood . . . Woodkkkk . . ." He got no further. My name again a source of hilarity.

"Well fellas," he continued in his tasteless joking, "I've heard tell of a 'wooden heart' but never a wooden co . . . co . . . k . . . k . . ."

Gerald didn't laugh with them. The red flecks in his jacket were really very striking. He gave me a long, slow look. I felt so out of control, I wanted to run away. But there was no corner I knew of here, no bolt-hole like my little farm.

"That's really hard luck, Philippa," he said. "I could cheerfully put his mike somewhere really painful."

The thought of Mr Kearney experiencing electric shocks cheered me up.

I smiled my thanks. Lest he felt I was up for grabs, I decided the evening had come to an end.

"I must be going. It was a long journey and I need a little rest before I have the energy to enjoy myself."

He looked crestfallen. I immediately regretted what I'd said.

"Well, if that's what you want, of course. If it's not too cheeky of me to say so, I'll miss you."

That really got to me. Typical of you, Philippa, I thought, you find a decent man and you decide to go to your bed. Alone.

"Perhaps we'll meet at breakfast. I understand we're neighbours," he smiled that smile.

"Knowing these old farmhouses, you could probably spit peas through the walls."

And knowing how I snore, you'll probably be kept awake all night and not find me your favourite person in the morning.

But I left him to his illusions. After all, he may have too many whiskeys to hear anything.

Before I could beat my retreat, the band struck up a dance tune. Mr and Mrs Kearney were leading the floor.

Everyone moved their chair to watch them. I was even tapping a surreptitious foot myself. Several more couples got up. What a motley crew they were. Tinker-pink jumpers abounded, large white plastic beads hopped in the air and beat against chins. Trousers became unstuck and slipped an inch or two below bulges of fat; sleeves went up to reveal white, hairy arms.

Another drink was placed in my hand. The Kearneys were riveting, tearing around the room, bumping into pieces of furniture, Mrs Kearney's vast bulk swaying like a ship on choppy waters. Occasionally they were joined by other natives, easily spotted by their hair, reddish-brown curled wire, growing at a slant like a Fukinagashi-style bonsai, all the foliage borne in the lee.

I sipped at my drink and really I felt I'd had enough but swallowed it graciously so as not to offend. Gerald asked me for the next dance. How could I refuse?

We swirled and bumped and slipped like the rest of them. I felt hot and dizzy. The room seemed set on a slope.

Smoke caught my throat. I excused myself. Gerald followed close on my heels. There was no time to dissuade him. Out I had to get.

Of course as soon as the cold air hit me, I thought I'd collapse. The room had been much too hot and all that prancing around wasn't such a good idea.

I needed to lie down. Immediately, if not sooner. A stretch of grass chose me before I had time to make a decision. The cool wetness of it against my face was heaven. I must have dozed off for a bit for the next I knew Gerald and several other people were chattering and pulling at me. I was quite happy where I was, thank you, I wanted to say but no one was listening. It was like being in one of those dreams where you're trying desperately to explain something and the words won't come. I recognised Sean Kearney's voice.

"Come on up now, me girl, we'll have you between nice clean sheets in next to no time. It's a bit on the cold side to be lying here by the side of the road and the autumn mists playing about your ears."

For a horrifying minute I thought he said something really rude. Poor Mrs Kearney was all solicitude, going ahead to light our way with a torch and talking about a hot-water bottle.

It was all so unnecessary. I was perfectly all right if they would all just mind their own business. Somewhere to have a little rest was all I needed. But that was not to be. When we reached the house, they insisted on bringing me upstairs.

"A cup of coffee and a little chat is all I need," I tried to explain but it came out peculiarly. Sometimes it's easier to give in.

To my consternation Sean Kearney went the whole hog and brought me upstairs. I was alarmed at the thought of the inevitable disrobing and decided to take firm action. I had been lily-livered up to now. I stood squarely in the door frame and said in my most commanding voice, "That's perfectly all right now; I'll manage the rest."

Unfortunately, my legs went a trifle rubbery and I had a tremendous urge to sit down. As one, they grabbed at me, Mr and Mrs Kearney, Gerald (much to my annoyance) and a "wire hair" I had seen earlier.

My face soon hit the delicious crispness of the pillow, with its scent of salt and meadowsweet. Mr Kearney mentioned something about two boiled aspros for breakfast and I fell fast asleep.

Which is what I had been trying to do all along but no one listened.

I awoke early with a ferocious headache. Overtiredness no doubt. The blue sheet of sea was the first thing I saw. I felt better immediately. I wanted to feel it, to capture it. All very silly. Beauty cannot be captured and held. Its sadness derives from that fact. It cannot be taken in and digested like a steak and kidney pie.

There wasn't a sinner up. All collapsed from their prancing around the previous night. I put on my wax jacket and gloves and took a plastic bag with me in case I fell upon some wild mushrooms. Nothing better for a sore head.

In no time I was at Dun Aengus. I would be able to regale the girls at home about its glories, although Noreen had done the trip last year. The chevaux de frise are magnificent. What a barrier to intruders! The idea ought to be taken up, not to mention a pot of boiling oil from a bedroom window. We've become too civilised, too full of human kindness. No wonder we're easy meat for anyone who's in need of cash. One could devise very subtle chevaux de frise, hidden amongst the snow-in-summer and delphiniums . . .

"My goodness, I didn't think we'd see you this side of Christmas!"

I almost fell upon the jagged tooth of rock. It was Gerald. I didn't like his astonished exclamation.

"Nothing like a breath of sea air to clear the lungs," I said, staring out to sea.

We stood in the inner circle and looked around.

"They say it was built as a place of refuge," he said picking up a stone.

"They do, though I'm afraid I don't subscribe to that notion at all. For a start there is no water to sustain occupation for any length of time and secondly, why build chevaux de frise on that side when your enemy would certainly come from the other?"

"But why build all the walls if not for defence?" he said throwing the stone into the air and deftly catching it.

"As you are probably aware, walls are for keeping things in as well as out. In this case, they were to keep in animals of some sort which were then selected for sacrifice and brought to this altar here."

"But my book says this altar is nothing but a piece of natural rock." He threw the stone down the cliff to the swirling sea.

"Pay no attention to books, Gerald. Most writers haven't a clue what they're talking about. They never really look. They never accept the simplest explanation. Yes, it's a natural piece of rock but what better choice for an altar? It saves you making one. Even early man was as lazy as we are. We only ever do anything when our back's to the wall."

"That's a pretty cynical view, Philippa. I think man is always striving, constantly trying to better himself."

"I grant you man may wish to better himself but he's too damn lazy to actually do what needs to be done."

Such a relief to be on holiday and voice my opinion.

"What do you mean, Philippa, 'needs to be done'?"

"Change, Gerald, change. That's everyone's greatest fear and if they but knew it, the source of their deepest joy."

He looked at me in the way men used to do. Half fear, half deference.

"I think I know what you mean. Change is difficult. And you, Philippa, are an extraordinary woman and, if I may be so bold as to say it, very beautiful."

For once I was flummoxed. I stopped to see if he meant it, looked right into his eyes. And I trembled at what I saw. But it was all so silly, ridiculous. It was time we were getting back.

We parted at Mrs Kearney's. I decided I needed some time to get myself sorted out. I wandered back up the road in the opposite direction, towards Onaght with its seven churches. The last resting place of St Enda and his monks, their once adventurous and hopeful bodies now dust. Like myself one day. There was a chill in the air. I thought of my farmhouse nestling against the little green hill, the chickens, ducks, Nanny with her growing kid and Poppy with her calf. Someone to mourn their passing and no one to notice mine.

"Sure we thought you'd been swept off by the ghosties that haunt the church up there," Mrs Kearney's chest wobbled an admonishment.

"Come on now and get a dish of soup into you and you won't know yourself."

"Don't worry at all, Mrs Kearney. You can't kill a bad thing."

"That's for certain," Mr Kearney said, looking meaningfully in his wife's direction. Married bliss strikes again.

In the dining-room, I looked around for Gerald.

"If it's himself you're after, then I'm afraid he's gone to the mainland."

Stabbed, I lurched towards the table. Best not to let it show.

"A very nice man," she continued, "quite the gentleman."

A gentleman would at least have said good-bye, like any normal person. What a slug!

After the soup came a thick brown stew, studded with rounds of carrot, accompanied by freshly dug potatoes. I would have eaten it from the floor it was so good.

A beaming Mr Kearney delivered the tea. He had obviously done a very careful job of washing his hands which were white as far as could be seen until he stretched his arm to reveal skin that hadn't seen water since pussy was a cat. Poor Mrs Kearney. Emily's woes with Dickie and his marrows were as nothing compared to this.

"Bring the tea over to the fire and we'll have a little chat," Mrs Kearney encouraged. She settled down with her knitting, a baby's cardigan in marshmallow pink.

She nodded towards the kitchen.

"One lives in hope," she whispered, holding up the tiny cardigan. "I've said that many devotions and novenas. I even went to Lough Derg. Not even the pepper tea or torn feet did a bit of good."

I was tempted to inform her that it takes penance of a different sort to make a baby, but I held back. The opportunities one lets slip sometimes.

"I'm probably too old now. As the doctor told me, 'All the little eggs may be past their sell-by date'. But sure, God is good. Didn't John the Baptist's mother have him and her in her sixties."

At the kitchen door, I watched as Mr Kearney's shadow lifted a hand and rubbed its head.

So the cock had lost its crow.

The sea air must have gone for me. I dozed off on the settee and woke to see Mr and Mrs Kearney in the kitchen, having a tête-à-tête. Mrs Kearney handed back to her husband, one by one, the freshly dried crockery, pointing at bits he'd obviously missed when he washed them. She spoke in Irish, words coming ninety to the dozen. Just when it seemed the matter was over with and Mrs Kearney dried her hands, some fury possessed her. She lifted her fist and landed a hefty thump in the middle of Mr K's back.

I quickly shut my eyes, feigning sleep. Another happy couple. Six more days of this would be unendurable. And Gerald gone. I felt as lonely as I did in Paris, having left my beloved Jack at the local hospital, dying from blood poisoning.

But none of this would get me anywhere. I got up and went to my room. Having read two pages of Muriel Spark's life story, I dozed off.

It was still light when a noise at the door woke me up. Not Mr Kearney, I hoped, however harmless he seemed to be. Perhaps Mrs Kearney doing her good Samaritan bit. It opened a crack.

"Philippa?"

Gerald!

"Are you awake?"

Not only awake but bolt upright, trying to fix my hair and rub some colour into my cheeks. The bottle of Madame Rochas was just out of reach. I would stink of sleep.

"Mind if I come in?"

"Of course," I squeaked, pretending more relaxation than I felt, unfolding and uncurling as he entered the room, like a flower at dawn.

I mentioned nothing of his departure.

"I was over on the mainland, Philippa. Picked this up. Care to join me?" He held out a distinctly champagne-like shape wrapped in tissue paper.

"The only way to drink champagne is in the comfort of

33

one's bed." Fully clothed of course, I didn't add.

He produced two crystal goblets. A man of taste. In fact those red flecks really made that jacket.

He looked around for a seat. Not a spare chair in sight. To hell with it. I patted the bed. He leapt onto it like a ballerina. Our legs touched. I felt that jelly feeling again and scolded myself. He's only a man, after all.

"What a good idea," I said, original as anything.

"Well, I fancied a little something to celebrate. My editors have accepted my latest offering."

"That must be a very nice feeling, like when Poppy or Nanny have safely given birth."

"Well, yes. I was worried about this one because it was a new departure, a mystery set in the twelfth century. They prefer them to be up to the minute, full of sex and blood."

"It's nice that it worked out for you."

He popped the cork out the window and began to pour.

"Well, cheers, Philippa," he said, offering me a glass. "Here's to a new friendship."

He seemed so honest and straightforward, I wanted to agree but I couldn't. The treachery of the past was still with me.

"Of course, Gerald. It's very nice knowing you."

By the time the bottle was finished, I felt quite at ease with the world. My previous desire to escape had evaporated. Gerald and I were now a cosy twosome, propped against the pillows, reciting poetry to each other. He recited Donne so beautifully, I almost cried. Champagne tears. Touched, he leaned towards me and dried them with his lips. His mouth was warm and soft against my cheeks. Legs pressed against me and soon his body was so close, so pressed, as if glued. I could smell him now, spicy, manly. The first button on his shirt was undone, exposing his neck to me, a neck of smooth skin and dark corners ending in powerful shoulders whose arms could hold and press and . . . I remembered just in time that I had my plain knickers on and not the lacy jobs I had for special occasions. As if stung, I jumped from the bed.

"My goodness," I said with a touch of breathlessness, "champagne's the divil. Mustn't flout Mrs K's religious scruples. I'm sure you've seen the BVM and the little light burning for dear life in the hallway."

I knew he wasn't listening. But I gabbled on to fill the void.

I stuck my head out the window.

"Oh," I breathed deeply, "you can taste the salt. Isn't it wonderful to feel so much part of that huge expanse that you can taste it on your lips. I just love the sea. Look, there's the last boat coming in with another influx. I wonder who's in store for us tonight."

Thought of the future might take his mind off things. But as I turned, I saw the heel of his shoe disappear out the door. So much for men. Who needs them anyway? It's all so complicated. They expect so much.

The dining-room was full to the gills when I went down. Gerald was there, in the far corner, talking animatedly to the people at his table. So much for bruised feelings. He obviously had a layer of rubber around his heart.

"Where'll I put you now, Miss Woodcock?" Mrs Kearney looked around the room, her eye lighting in consternation on Gerald's already full table.

"It's perfectly all right, Mrs K, don't worry," I said, making for a table with a man and a woman staring glumly into space. Obviously tourists: tanned and well-fed looking.

"Wonderful weather for this time of year," I began earnestly. Silence.

"Enjoying your holiday?" A smile from the man.

"All so quaint. Untouched." I'm sure he meant unspoilt. Definitely French, I decided.

"Paris?"

"From birth, yes. But in retreat at Aix-en-Provence."

"It must be wonderful to be retired. Your time your own."

Madame gave a little cough.

"Except that Monsieur 'as too much time," she sniffed.

Monsieur shuffled his feet. A suppressed kick. Trust me to land myself among happy families again.

"I expect one gets used to it," I said, pouring oil as usual. "And how is Aix? I have such wonderful memories of it."

The tree-lined boulevard where Jack, a Rhodes scholar, and I sat in the afternoons, too warm to do any more work in the University Library.

"Aix is very expensive," Monsieur continued as Madame pursed her lips. "Even more after Paris. *Très bourgeois*."

Full of lawyers, doctors and rich civil servants. A little short on artists these days since the demise of Cézanne.

"We even have a baron."

"Of course, I remember. Baron de Montremontant, lived near the Mont St Victoire, produced wine."

Did I remember! Saturday afternoons he came down from his château to sit in his favourite café. If he happened to talk to you and liked the look of you, you were invited to the château that evening.

Jack and I went. "You never pass up a free meal," was Jack's philosophy. The table was at least twenty feet long, piled with food. Each dish hid something completely different. However, I let the side down with my little yelp when they opened the casserole of little song birds. We were never invited back.

"He is very *bizarre* now." Madame bent forward. "Has young girls living with him." I seemed to remember he had a reputation. There is no such thing as a free dinner. Or even a free glass of champagne. I glanced over at Gerald.

36

He happened to look at me too. I pretended I was having a whale of a time and laughed at nothing.

By the time the apple tart and cream arrived, I was thoroughly fed up with my companions at the trough. Every morsel they ate was commented upon. It was either a bit on the overdone side or too moist or, most often, *pas extraordinaire*.

That about summed them up. The only problem I ever found with France was that it was full of French people.

Mrs Kearney arrived at my side, panting.

"A phone call, Miss Woodcock. Down in the hall."

Who on earth knew I was here? Emily, of course.

"Philippa," said Emily at the other end, "bad news. Nanny has escaped and some careless motorist has run over one of your queer hens."

"Not the Silkie!"

"Afraid so. Will I bury it for you, or would you rather . . ."

"You do the necessary, Emily. Except, if you wouldn't mind, keep a few of the tail-feathers for me."

They're very nice in an arrangement. May as well salvage something.

"What about Nanny? It's her little kids I'm really worried about. They're beside themselves with anguish."

"Don't worry about them. They're not weaned at this stage, so Nanny wouldn't just dump them. Give them a cabbage to worry about."

I suddenly realised how much I was enjoying myself and didn't really want to bother about Nanny.

"Never mind about Nanny either. She's used to fending for herself. Probably gone off to find a billy."

"Found one yourself, Philippa?"

Emily can be trying at times. However, no point in creating bad feeling.

"Not a goat in sight, Emily. But coming down with cattle and sheep. You'd love it."

"I'm sure," was all she said.

"Oh, by the way, the woman with the cleft palate phoned again."

I had to think for a minute. Of course, it was Agatha. I told everyone she had a cleft palate but the slurring was really due to ten gins too many. But no point in shocking Emily. This was serious indeed. Half of Agatha's liver was in shreds.

"Did she leave a number?"

"She said you'd get her at the usual place."

The clinic for gin-sodden rich folk. Those with no VHI languish in the back wards of St Brendan's, their brains the size of a walnut.

I would have to break short my holiday. The problem with Agatha was she was my sister and I loved her.

Over tea in the sitting-room, I told Mrs Kearney I'd be leaving in the morning.

She put aside the little cardigan.

"That's a shame, Miss Woodcock. I was looking forward to bringing you to see my relations on Inisheer. The brother's a fisherman and tells a great yarn and his wife has just been delivered of a new babby. But there ye are, if you've got to go that's it. Maybe some other time."

"I look forward to that." I almost meant it, in spite of the slap I witnessed in the kitchen. Gerald came in.

"Mr Ransome, hang on a minute and I'll get you a fresh cup," Mrs Kearney lifted the teapot and ran to the kitchen. Gerald sat next to me. I noticed his hands, long slim fingers with beautiful nails resting across the top of his thighs.

I smiled my most appealing smile and he returned it. To hell with it. I'll tell the truth for once. We may never see each other again.

"I enjoyed meeting you, Gerald. I liked your company very much."

"But not my body," he said rather quickly and then,

38

"Indeed, I enjoyed yours too. I'd like to see more of you," he said meaningfully.

I took it in good part. Life was too short to take offence. After all, there was Agatha with half a liver.

"For the present, that may not be possible. I have to return tomorrow. One of the family is ill. Nothing serious, just a relapse."

Silence and then the bustle of Mrs Kearney.

"Here you are, Mr Ransome. I bet your tongue's hanging out for it. Nothing like a sup of tea to wash the dinner down with."

She poked at the fire and heaped it with sods of turf.

"There now. That should keep the evening chill at bay while I'm away dancing off a few pounds in Dillon's." She gave me an enormous wink and left the room. Everyone had gone except Mr Kearney, still in the kitchen, scrubbing away for all he was worth.

"So, is this goodbye or do we exchange addresses to send each other Christmas cards?"

"Whatever you wish, Gerald." I felt a bit irritated at the finality of his sentiments.

"Put like that," he said sipping his tea, "what I wish is to see you again. How about coming over to see me for a few days? I'll start my next book as soon as I return and should be well on just in a few weeks."

"You can fit me in then, is that it?" It came out so quickly, there was no chance to stop it. A lot to be said for speaking as slowly as an American, you can think at least two sentences ahead.

"It would be a pleasure," he said smiling.

"I can't think straight just now. Perhaps you would get in touch later."

Perhaps a few days home would cool his ardour or whet his appetite. It remained to be seen.

Sean Kearney came into the room, pulling down his

sleeves and drying his hands along the side of his trousers. He declined Gerald's invitation to go to the pub and sat opposite me in the over-stuffed armchair.

"So, it's Ballinamore you're from. A grand little town beside the Slieve Blooms."

"You know it, Mr Kearney?"

"Sure I'm certain you've heard tell of a cousin of mine, married to a Shorthall, living in the Square."

It was double dutch to me.

"What's his first name?" I asked through clenched teeth.

"Seamus, Seamus Mulready."

I couldn't believe my ears but then it fitted like a puzzle. Noreen's Seamus and Sean Kearney were two of a kind.

"Of course," was all I could manage.

At least poor Noreen managed to have children but then Noreen has character. Hidden shallows.

Sean fiddled with the fire, poking at the burning turf and sending out puffs of ash. Mrs K wouldn't be too pleased. He seemed to want to talk but could find nothing to say. His head sunk lower and lower into his chest. The "hail fellow, well met" jollity had dissipated. I was terrified that some momentous revelations were to be unfolded. I really didn't want to know. Men seem to think women have a ready ear for that sort of thing.

"Grand clutch of childer they have. Grand clutch." He flopped back into the chair, startling the remaining loose ash. His hands slid under his large belly, cradling it.

"I suppose it's all His will," he said glancing heavenwards.

With a little help from down here, I felt like adding but didn't. One thing I learned during my mad days with the Samaritans is that no one wants to hear your tuppenceworth when they're telling you theirs. One thing certain to make the suicide take the fatal jump is the voice of a know-it-all at the other end of the phone.

"It would be grand all the same to have a few little gossoons gadding about, playing at the edge of the water, stuffing theirselves with hunks of bread and jam and falling asleep by the fire," he said as his shoulders collapsed in on him and his head sunk even lower on his chest. His large, worn hands rubbed the big fold of his belly.

We gazed into the embers for a while longer. I stretched and stood up.

"Well it's beddybyes for me, Mr K. Good-night."

"And a goodnight to you Miss Woodcock. And, by the way, I just want to say it wasn't in the best of taste. You know, my joking about your name."

I'd almost forgotten but now that he mentioned it, it was at the edge of my awareness of him.

"When a fella gets a few pints inside him, he gets a bit silly. No offence meant, at all. No offence."

"And none taken," I said, more enlightened than I cared to be about his little problem. As someone once said, to understand is to forgive. So boring.

I rinsed out the champagne glasses and packed my bag. I didn't bother with breakfast in case the crossing was rough, although the seagulls might have been grateful for any offerings on the cold, grey day.

On the little wash-stand I left a note for the Kearneys and had a quick scarper to Teampall Chiaráin. The same Kieran who founded Clonmacnoise and whose namesake, Kieran of Saighir, founded Saighir Kieran where the girls and I had such a wonderful evening. Perhaps all the best people come to Aran to be renewed and fortified for the journey ahead, like St Brendan and his monks before they took off for America in their boat of oxhides to live off birds and whales.

The ferry was practically empty; one old codger sat inside out of the wind. At least I wouldn't have to bother making polite conversation to anyone.

Just as we were about to leave, a group of people made their way down the pier towards the boat. I spotted the noble head of Gerald. Even Mr Kearney was there. Did I forget something? Was something missing? Mrs Kearney shouted, "We wanted to see you off, Miss Woodcock. And thank you for the nice present." She was referring to the small gift I'd left for her.

"Have a good journey. Come back to us again." This from a smiling Sean.

Gerald said nothing. He simply looked. As the boat drew away, he threw a bunch of wild flowers at me. They fell short and landed on the water, to drown in the boat's oily wake.

A dismal feeling stayed with me until I got home. However, the sight of Nanny, as she poked her head out of the shed and gave me a little whimper of welcome, cheered me up. In no time I had made myself a hot whiskey, lit the fire and turned on the electric blanket. I lay in bed, listening to a play about a woman's house burning down, killing her only child. I suddenly felt content, that I was snug and warm in my bed with its crisp linen sheets and the hot whiskey warming and comforting me. Pleased also that not a thought of Gerald had crossed my mind. I had no intention of becoming a Marianne pining for her Willoughby.

Sleep is such a wonderful thing if it weren't for the dreams. Drowning flowers begging to be rescued.

Agatha was over her withdrawal symptoms, so I paid her a visit. St Jude's nestled at the foot of the Dublin mountains; a luxurious shelter of plush carpets, gourmet food and fresh air – the sort of place where you can gather your wits in some comfort. The rest of the world has to do the best it can at home.

The inmates had faces as long as a wet week. No doubt they believed they had a monopoly on suffering. They should try farming.

This time Agatha was in a poor state, having been found at the end of her garden, collapsed over a hole she'd been digging. Her neighbour phoned to tell me all about it. I really didn't want to know. However, there is no escape from the bond that is sisterhood. I listened.

"I'm very worried about her," Mrs Gilligan whispered as if Agatha were at her elbow. "She's been quite strange recently. And she told Thomas and I that she was very depressed. So, on Thursday or maybe Wednesday night, I can't remember which because we have our own troubles – I don't know if Agatha told you, our young son is having an operation to save his eyes. We can think of nothing else."

Just what I needed. An earful of more misery. I really do wish people would keep it to themselves. I was still trying to recover from Sean Kearney's belly.

"I'm sure," was all I said.

"So, Thomas was outside, letting the dog have its

evening walk. If he doesn't have it we have this unholy mess in the morning. Anyway, he just happened to look over the fence and there was Agatha digging for all she was worth. A stack of clay to one side and herself standing in the hole, with only a head showing."

Perhaps she was planning one of those stand-up burials. Or emigrating to Australia to join the brother.

"Thomas asked whether everything was okay and she just said, 'Perfectly, thank you.' But it bothered him. He couldn't drink his Ovaltine and didn't take his Moggy in case, you know, just in case he was needed. So, in the heel of the hunt, he was doing his exercises in front of the window and happened to look out and saw her, Agatha that is, and she lying on top of the mound of clay. And I'm sorry to have to say this, there's no easy way to put it – she hadn't a stitch on."

This was a new departure. The gin was obviously doing its worst in the primitive department. They say we all want to get back to the cosiness of the womb. However, it would be useless to tell her what she had done in the garden, she just wouldn't believe me. She would tell her shrink how cracked I was. I had no intention of submitting myself to their scrutiny. From what I had heard about them, they seemed a little on the crazy side themselves. If you keep a horse, chances are you'll end up looking like one.

Lying back on her sick-bed, surrounded by pastel walls and bouquets of flowers, Agatha explained what brought on this latest "attack of depression".

"There was a poor fellow I met who has AIDS, Pippy. I just felt so down I had to have a few drinks."

From what the doctor had told me, a few gallons was more likely.

A nurse came in with a bright yellow pill and glass of water. She stood there while Agatha took it. As soon as she'd gone, Agatha spat it out.

"That's the one they give you at night, in case you feel like escaping. Designed to make you drop like a stone as soon as fresh air hits you."

"Perhaps you need it – to help you sleep."

"You couldn't sleep here if they knocked you out with a sledgehammer. There are some really peculiar people. A man who thinks he's Che Guevara, complete with black cap. I really think it's vanity, trying to hide his bald pate. And then there's a woman whose poodle was run over by a steam-roller."

The whole gamut of human emotions from A to B. If it weren't for the VHI the place would be empty.

"Surely the loss of a dog, even a poodle, wouldn't cause that much anguish," I protested.

"Apparently the dear little thing had been left in the care of her sister and was mown down when on its morning run. When she arrived back and was told the bad news, the poor woman lost the head and took a bread knife to her sister."

That put a different complexion on it. Insanity was preferable to being behind bars.

I was offered tea and a piece of fruitcake. "No nuts," Agatha said, attempting to be light-hearted. We sipped in silence. I really wanted to shout at her, tell her to cop on to herself, that the only problem she had came out of a bottle. But it was useless. She just wouldn't believe it, so I kept my mouth shut.

"AA paid me another visit, Pippy. Really, it's not my cup of tea. I told them I just wasn't interested."

I decided it was time to go. I had heard nothing new. Agatha was still wrapped up in herself, still refused to accept she had a disease.

I suddenly felt very lonely. A goldfish would be better company. It would have been nice to have been asked about my holiday.

In the corridor, bodies passed me, eyes glazed, oblivious to everything. No need for straitjackets any more. The chemicals did the job just as well. The silence was eerie. I'd have been happier if people behaved more normally, screamed and tore their hair out, had a good cry. But no. Keep it under wraps was the message.

Agatha saw me off at the door, watched by a man in uniform, his fingers hovering over a bank of buttons, ready to call up who knows what army of medics, syringes at the ready.

"It's so depressing here," she said, "they want you to take up knitting or embroidery."

"I suppose the idea is your hands are so busy they haven't time to get at the gin."

She bridled at this and slammed the door.

Autumn stole up unawares. A distinct chill set in. I stacked up a heap of turf just inside the back door. I kept busy filling my orders for chutney, apple jelly and cranberry sauce for Christmas. It brought in a few ducats to buy a turkey and a bottle of château-bottled wine. I am spared the torment of a mortgage, having bought the farm outright with my father's stamp album. Unknown to him, his schoolboy album I kept in his memory contained a rare tuppenny blue and an exotic Cape of Good Hope triangular, uncancelled on an envelope.

A note arrived from Gerald and lay unopened on the dresser. I looked at it every time I passed, hoping I would just grab at it and open it. But I couldn't. I was being so silly. At least he hadn't forgotten. I was cross at being so delighted. Cross that I couldn't just open the thing. Cross that I cared. And then cross for being cross.

After milking Nanny and locking up the hens against foxy loxy, I poured a stiff brandy with soda. Not gin. That's what did it for Agatha.

I could see the envelope out of the corner of my eye, blue with a bright stamp, neat yet artistic, almost flamboyant writing. However, my cross-stitch was at a crucial stage. The very tip of the parsnip had to be accomplished very delicately or it would appear deformed. After a second brandy and on completion of the parsnip, I simply picked up the envelope and matter-of-factly sat down. So far so good.

> *Dear Philippa,*
> *I rescued the flowers that fell into the water. They washed up on the beach next day. Dried them off and gave them to Mrs Kearney – she said she'd keep them for you.*
> *I trust the nanny goat was found before too much damage was done. I'd forgotten to put my plants onto their capillary matting. They're very sad-looking. A bit like myself – would love to meet you again. Aran seems so far away.*
> *Warmest regards,*
> *Gerald*

To my chagrin, I jumped up and down and got dizzy. The brandy probably. No point in seeming too eager, like a Sheela-na-Gig. Stay calm, cool and collected. We probably would never see each other again. I certainly wouldn't go out of my way to arrange it. But oh, joy! Oh, bliss! Even if it were the devil himself, isn't it wonderful to be desired!

"You're back. I thought we'd lost you for good!" Hope springs eternal. It was Clara of the Archaeological Society on the phone.

"It was hardly a week, Clara." Clara is terrified I'll find a man before she does. She thinks herself a better catch, being a nurse. Farmers seem seduced by the notion that a nurse will look after them and their animals better than anyone. They don't realise their job teaches them detachment, renders their heart like steel.

"Anything interesting happen?"

"Of course. Aran is always magical." I enjoy teasing her.

"What's his name?"

"Well, I stayed with Mr and Mrs Kearney. A lovely couple. Couldn't do enough for me."

"No eligible bachelors then?"

"And the weather was terrific. And Dun Aengus was wonderful."

"You'll have to tell us all about it," she said, a trifle insincerely, I felt. "Our next meeting is Monday. In Claffey's to organise the winter schedule."

"I'll do my best to be there. You'll have to excuse me, Clara; there's a casserole going dry."

"You've heard about Gaye Greene? They say she's found a boyfriend. She was seen holding hands with him in Bewley's."

"Could be a relative or even a friend."

"Perhaps they were just feeling the cold. How silly of me."

I wished I could have said, please don't be hurt and angry with me. Let's begin again. But it was pointless. The deeper you go, the thicker the muck. So I said nothing. One of these days . . .

Autumn is the busiest time of year. The vegetables have to be lifted and clamped. Not the easiest thing to do. Mr Rat is always on the prowl. Nothing is so maddening as to discover his sharp teeth marks in the turnips and potatoes. So I usually make an elaborate structure that not even a snail could pass. I dig a pit and line it with chicken wire. A layer of straw goes on top of this and then a skin of clay, well battened down.

The straw is a bit of a problem because I don't produce my own – I'm not brave enough to grow some wheat or barley. I have an aversion to using chemical sprays and I would be frightened I'd lose the whole crop to some exotic fungus disease. So I give my neighbour, PJ, a few jars of my preserves and he drops off a few bales of straw. The only difficulty is how to get rid of the man.

"What do you want to be growing your own potatoes and carrots for? A bag costs no more than a few pounds. Instead of creasing yourself with work," he looked at me appraisingly. At this stage, five years on, he's stopped wondering why I bought a farm on my own. I'm part of the landscape now, albeit a strange, peculiar corner.

Several cups of tea and a few oatcakes later, he was gone, leaving a little pile of dried mud on my quarry tiles. Perhaps I should think of growing some barley next year.

There is a pleasure in growing vegetables that PJ does not understand. Watching them grow from fuzzy little specks of green into feathery fronds with bright red roots going deeply into the soil is ecstasy. To lift them, an hour before dinner, a quick rub with a brush and taste them as they were meant, is magic. No vegetable was meant to live for days and days in a plastic bag. Who wouldn't be gone off after that!

Then, of course, the freezer has to be filled before the onset of winter and the job I hate most has to be performed. The little lambs I have watched over, healed when sick, sat up nights worrying about, are given the chop. It's a betrayal I haven't resolved. From a practical point of view, if I were to keep them, they would die anyway as I haven't enough winter feed.

"Why have them in the first place?" Agatha remarked one time we were tucking into a casserole of little Lily the Lamb.

"Well, I have rationalised it thus. If I am to have a decent diet and do justice to the pasture I have, I need to keep sheep. The cow will eat the long grass but sheep will

49

crop it closer, causing it to tiller, so you don't get gaps in the pasture, there's better photosynthesis, and so an optimum environment for all the worms and bugs under the soil."

"My God, Pippy, you sound like a walking encyclopaedia. Why you bother with all that verbiage beats me."

"You sound just like mother. The reason I bother with it, Agatha, is because I enjoy it. Some people prefer watching paint dry or gin bottles empty. That is up to them. I don't interfere."

Happy families. They'd put you off people for life. Probably why I prefer animals. Take Nanny, for instance. She's her own person. She has her likes and dislikes, her set routines, her favourite bushes, even her own spot against the garden wall where she likes to sit and sunbathe. I often visit her there and stroke her. She opens a tiny slit of her eye and bends her head back against the wall. I feel she's telling me how much she likes me doing that, that life chez Pippy is the best there is. I would never mention that to anyone. They'd think I was mad.

Poppy, the cow, has her moments too. She's a terror when she has a calf. Always thinks I'm up to no good, about to steal it from her. And the calf plays up to her fears by yelling its head off. Then she snorts and paws the ground and pushes her great muzzle against me. However, when I take the calf from her to wean it and fatten it for the murder machine, she's back to her old self. The smell from her is the headiest mixture I know, a combination of milk and grass, slightly coconutty.

A holiday is out of the question until the ducks are killed and plucked and all the preserves have been made. In late October, I usually manage a week off.

It seemed about the right time to do that spinning course I had been promising myself for years. The fleeces had been piling high in the barn, ready to be spun. I fancied myself in a nice bhrat, a sort of coat they used to wear centuries ago.

I happened to spot just the course in one of the magazines Agatha had at the clinic. An indoor person, (fresh air gives her a headache), Aggie loves anything on interior design. She has some sort of diploma in it and according to herself, has a long list of clients who seek her advice. I always felt that part of Agatha's problem was she hadn't got a proper job. At a young age she went off to Saudi Arabia "to teach," she said. She came back with wads of money and jewellery with no explanation as to how she acquired it. I never asked.

The spinning course was in Bath, a bit far away but in these days of cheap fares and falling sterling, it would probably work out cheaper than one at home. I sent for the brochures. I doubted if I would have time to visit Gerald.

Claffey's pub was swirling with cigarette fumes and the smell of toasted cheese sandwiches. I sat beside Emily. She had bought a vodka and blackcurrant juice for me and was halfway through a babycham and brandy mixture my mind boggled at.

"Well, has Nanny settled down again?" she asked me.

"You know these women when they're on heat," I confided, sipping the sickly drink. "Nothing will stop them. She spent three days with the billy on Mrs Waterhouse's farm in Kilkenny. I presume he performed the necessary."

"Isn't nature queer all the same," Emily put her glass down on the dirty table. "Imagine being that desperate. But I suppose there'd be no jokes about nuns and cucumbers if there weren't these urges. They say men have urges but it looks like the women are just as bad!"

I noticed Noreen's Seamus out of the corner of my eye. I could have sworn he was eavesdropping.

"Well, Miss Woodcock, how was the air up at Dun Aengus? Give ye any bad thoughts?" he asked.

Like how to trip you up so that you bit your tongue and couldn't speak for weeks, but I didn't dignify him with a reply.

"I hear tell you ran into a relation of mine, once removed. Sitting on a gold mine those Kearneys are, with the B & B full all the time. Charging the Yanks through the nose for a bit of bacon and egg and an old cobbled dinner in the evening."

I felt myself rushing to Mrs Kearney's defence and held myself in check. Perhaps Seamus was simply mischief-making, looking for quotable quotes. I said nothing.

"A'course," he bent towards us conspiratorially, "they've a lot of bother getting rid of the empty champagne bottles the guests leave after them," he winked.

I obviously slipped up badly.

"You don't say?" I replied, sounding, I hoped, nonplussed. "Noreen with you?" I asked, to change the subject.

"Yep. And Clara. We travelled together. Cheap on petrol but costly on the drinks." I took a deep swallow of my gin and blackcurrant. Emily wriggled her foot, itching to kick someone.

"I'm going up for another, Philippa. Are you ready yet?" she asked.

I accepted, pushing a £5 note into her hand. Seamus shuffled off when he saw there was nothing to be gained.

On her return, I asked Emily whether she'd look after things for me while I was in Bath.

"Away again!"

"Well, it's not really 'away', it's work. I've been meaning to learn to spin for ages and just couldn't find the right course. You're sure you'll be able to look after things?"

"Of course. The children love seeing the animals. They feed the ducks while I milk Nanny. You know, you could get fond of that animal. She's very affectionate."

There's something very nice about Emily.

"As for Poppy and her calf, she's the most jealous mother I've ever seen. If it were a human, I'd say the calf will grow up with all sorts of complexes and mother-fixations. But then maybe she's doing what's right. There's so much rubbish talked about how to rear children. Sure if we just followed our instinct, they'd probably do better."

"You've got to keep your distance from them, all the same, otherwise you smother them. They have to be toughened up for the world, get the corners knocked off them," Clara said, squeezing in beside us, adding her tuppence worth. Clara certainly hadn't a corner left in her body. I prayed I would never have to depend on her ministrations. She probably feels death is a good thing.

"Well, girls, what's new?" Clara continued, oblivious to my recoiling.

"Good old Philippa is off on her travels again." I could have killed Emily.

"Oh, is she now. Isn't it well for some. And who's the lucky man?" Trust Clara to reduce everything to the lowest common denominator.

"Business, Clara dear, business."

Mrs Greene arrived, breathless and radiant. It must be true about a lover. Women don't have that glow for no reason.

"Sorry I'm late. Percy's friend. Chats non-stop," she smiled. "We'd better begin." She tapped a glass and the meeting began. Emily read the secretary's report, about two pages of the outings we had made with observations and recommendations to be passed on to the Board of Public Works. Noreen felt the Sheela-na-Gig should be removed from Saighir Kieran "for safe-keeping". The truth of the matter may have had something to do with her red face. Seamus said we should visit places like Lough Gur again, maybe stay overnight somewhere so that we could get in as many sites as possible. I wondered what he was up to. Clara felt perhaps we could go somewhere "foreign", like Greece or Italy. Perhaps she has a penchant for dark skins and brown eyes. She must be growing desperate at this stage. I kept quiet about Bath, although by the end of the evening I was sure everyone knew.

As with all meetings, nothing was finalised. But if I know Emily, she would write up the minutes as if the plans had been made and would go ahead. No one minds so long as something happens and they don't have to take responsibility for it. Emily and I would work something out. I mentioned to her that Eddie Henderson, whom she'd met at Lough Gur, was an expert on megalithic tombs. She wrote his phone number in her book.

It was past midnight when I climbed on my bicycle, a little unsteadily but then it was a damp evening. I said "good-night" to the Sergeant at the crossroads. He never breathalyses cyclists. Luckily my head had cleared by the time I reached the house so that I could deal with what met me. Two of the ducks had managed to get entangled in the electrified netting. Animals can be so stupid and not realise what you're doing for them is for their own protection. Though dead as doornails, their bodies were still warm. They would always feed the cats for a day or two. No sense in wasting anything.

Two letters in the post. A note from Agatha.

Dearest Sister,

They've done what they could for me, God bless them, so am leaving St Jude's today. Still feel down. However, my bonsai need me. Another downpour like we've had and they'll be finished. Thank you for the grapes – presumably your own and the jam. Found them when you'd left.

Much love,

Ag.

So, once again madness is loosed upon the world. How much more would poor old Aggie's liver take? The local off-licence will be pleased. They could count on at least a bottle of gin a day. Why she didn't buy a case of it at a time puzzled me. But then, I suppose that would be admitting she needed it. To be avoided at all costs.

And then the good news. A leaflet from the Holborne Craft Centre in Bath on the "most comprehensive course ever on spinning and dyeing." Ploughperson's lunch included. Evenings free or entertainment arranged. Just my *tasse de thé*. Everything organised; one didn't have to think. I booked immediately and set about finishing the last of the autumn chores.

I took off to the wood, my tiny chainsaw slung over my shoulder and my flask of decaffeinated coffee in my pocket. An ancient ash, nipped in the growing point when young, had produced several giant trunks. Over time, rain filled the centre of the cluster and gradually rotted the core. One of these trunks had fallen. Ash is my favourite for burning. It doesn't need to be too dry. Splits like butter. Goggles, gloves and saw guard in place. The noise is alleviated by handy little balls of wax I picked up in France to help me cope with Jack's snoring. You soften them in your hand and then insert them in your ear where they take on its shape.

In an hour, I had enough wood to last a few weeks. Poppy and Nanny came up to watch. The sheep stood a respectful distance. Not interested in human contact. Very sensible.

Nanny wanted a rub and Poppy breathed her milky breath on me.

They took off like the clappers as someone hove into view.

"I just followed the noise." Gaye Greene, light-hearted and glowing in the soft October air.

"Well, I'm not hiding from anyone," I said. Which is exactly what I've spent my life trying to do.

"Just on my way to visit a friend. Oh Pippy, I'm so happy."

No reason to call me Pippy, just the same.

"I want to thank you for your encouragement that time in the Slieve Blooms. It was you who said, 'It may not be too late.' It stuck in my mind, so when I met Dunkie, I was ready. He's absolutely wonderful."

Aren't they all, until the rot sets in and they expect you to tell them how to run their lives and then blame you when it goes wrong.

"Well, good for you," I said, as gushing as I could muster. Go with the tide. No need to put a dampener on things.

"I feel about nineteen again. You know, Pippy, I thought my life was over, without ever having, you know, experienced love fully and completely."

I knew exactly what she meant. I hoped she wouldn't elaborate.

"That must be very nice for you, Mrs Greene," I interrupted. "Would you ever mind passing me those few bits of wood. The work never seems to end. As soon as this is done, there's some silage to be made and fence-clearing to be done."

"I am sorry. Here's me interrupting you with my little preoccupations. I nearly forgot. Could you let me have half a dozen ducks and a turkey and some of your redcurrant jelly?"

"Yes to the ducks and jelly – it's very good with lamb – but no to the turkey. I don't do them. Big, ugly brutes. Difficult to despatch. I either pull the head right off or they're flapping about for ages with their necks only half pulled."

Poor Mrs Greene, I could see I'd upset her.

"Well, I won't hold you up," she said, swallowing

noisily. Look forward to seeing you at the next meeting. I almost missed the last one. Friends can be very demanding of one's time."

She scurried off, crashing into low-lying branches and snagging her tights on a blackthorn in her haste. Some people have no respect for the solitude of a wood and the creatures in it.

By nightfall, I had the limb of the ash tree sawn and chopped into pieces. I was looking forward to a stiff brandy and soda with perhaps a morello cherry or two. There was a crisp white burgundy to go with the chicken pie.

Life has its compensations, though I suppose, if I were to be brutally honest, I was a little envious of Mrs G.

The last of the elderberry wine was made. I always make this properly. That means removing every single stalk, so that the tannin in these doesn't sneak into the wine and ruin it. The yeast is vital too. I always use a port yeast and leave it for two years to mature. The last batch didn't last that long. With the casserole of Lily the Lamb, Agatha insisted on "trying" it.

"Don't be so damn mean, Pippy. There's no point in the stuff going to waste!"

I could have throttled her. I was so stung by the "mean" label, my voice caught in my throat. Within an hour, an entire gallon jar of the finest, though slightly immature, elderberry Château Philippa, trickled past Agatha's tonsils to wreak even more havoc on her liver. I gave her beans on toast for tea, which she hates but I felt she could do with the protein.

The apple jelly is not a favourite with Agatha, so I manage to hold onto it. Mine is always a delicate shade of pink, achieved by not over-boiling the fruit, merely simmering it for a day or two, allowing the juice to escape gently. What visitors and I don't scoff, I sell in the country markets for an absolute song. But that is how the producer is rewarded nowadays. The profit goes to fat, bald men in grey suits with laptop computers who have never visited a farm in their life. They haven't a clue what it's like to be up all night helping a ewe to lamb or a cow to calve. They no doubt feel you merely let nature take its course, all you do is let them roam about, eating grass and getting fat. If only it were so simple. No such thing as muck to the eyes, the rain dripping down the back of your neck, your toes frozen in rubber boots. Much less the agony of watching an animal go into the slaughterhouse, so trusting, healthy and beautiful and then watch it reappear, its little feet chopped off, minus its tail and head. They think it arrives in tins. They haven't gone through any agony of loss or guilt. No thought of gratitude to the animal, of an admission of betrayal. It's simply a commodity, like butter or cheese.

Of course, there are some animals even I could cheerfully strangle. Pigs, for instance, they can be very trying. The day they arrived is engraved on my memory.

Everything seemed to happen at once, as if nature saw a vacuum and felt it had to rush in with all cannons blazing. At the very moment the pigs arrived on the doorstep, the Health Inspector called. I had ordered the pedigree Saddleback pigs eighteen months previously, demand being so great there was a waiting-list. Would that things were so for my Jacob sheep. People generally only want them as pets.

I ushered the Health Inspector into the kitchen with a mug of steaming tea and some of Philippa's Pâté on toast.

"I'm sure you won't mind if I take a look?" he stated rather than asked, his shining fáinne matching the gleam in his eyes.

What could I say? Health Inspectors have the power of life and death over the small producer.

"Of course. Bring your tea and a stool. They're a special

breed – Saddlebacks. Take to the outdoors like a duck to water." He put his initialled briefcase on a chair and brought a stool and his cup of tea to the door to watch the fray.

The pig breeder was not far from porcine himself, portly and hyperactive; though the pigs didn't pick their nose the way he did.

"So, these are my little piggies," I said to him as he struggled from the car, smelling of *Eau de Porc*.

"They seem anxious to dismount," I commented in desperation to get some sort of human response from him.

"Haven't eaten for three hours. Bound to be hungry."

Probably why he was picking his nose; breakfast was a memory.

"If you reverse in here, there's a cosy stall waiting."

Rule number one, if there's a new animal on the farm keep it where it cannot escape until the beast gets used to you and the new smells. Otherwise they'll go through barbed wire to get "home". Just like the rest of us.

Eau de Porc slithered into the car again with the practised ease of a limbo dancer and reversed into the stall.

With the rattle of the trailer door, the pigs squealed at the top of their lungs. Two seconds later, the door was flat on the ground and a mass of black with pink stripes shot to freedom. The boisterousness was something new, nothing like bovine placidity or ovine standoffishness. This was teenagers on the rampage after a dose of too much tartrazine in their orange juice.

I could have sworn I heard a chuckle at my back from the Health Inspector. I didn't have time to look as I ran towards the left to block the pigs' exit from the yard and the shortest "hello" in history. *Eau de Porc* was extricating himself from behind the steering wheel and taking a lot longer than I thought was necessary. A ton of pork was about to disappear down the road.

"Can I help?" the Inspector asked, his fáinne glinting like mad.

"Of course," I said through gritted teeth, "if you see a pig, perhaps you'd be kind enough to catch it."

They were almost at the end of the yard now. Just as they were about to turn the corner, *Eau de Porc* rattled a bucket and like trained greyhounds, back they came, ears flying, snouts in the air. Quick as a flash, the nuts were deposited on the ground and gobbled up with great snorts of something or another.

I thanked God there was something they responded to.

"They know the way to their mouths anyway," the Inspector said with considerable insight.

"Sensible animals, pigs," *Eau de Porc* stated. "No messing about. Just tuck right in."

None of the other animals would have been able to cope with these rough, rude things. Fortunately, I made a special paddock for them, complete with wallowing hole and straw-lined arks. Getting them there would be quite a feat. I was torn between taking advantage of the help available or shutting them out of harm's way as soon as possible. I decided on the latter. No sense in taking chances with the Inspector.

"Well, I'll settle up with you, *Eau de* . . . I mean, I don't think we've had the pleasure."

I stuck my hand out and got my fingers crushed.

"O'Dea. Been in pigs all my life, though my wife does the day-to-day running of the place. I do all the paperwork."

A little exercise wouldn't hurt, but I kept quiet.

"Speaking of which, I probably owe you some money."

I ran for a cheque, signed it and wished him good-bye.

"Of course, if they drop dead within the week, I'll be in touch," I said to his back as he slid into the car once more.

"Chirpy little fellows," the Inspector said, brushing the

last of the toast crumbs from a mouth that seemed too sensual for someone who wore a fáinne. "The 'gentleman that pays the rent', the pig was always known as in times gone by."

"Is that so?" I said, as if hearing the little nugget of priceless information for the first time. The truth was I'd a headache from hearing that every time I mentioned pigs. I can be as hypocritical as the next when it comes to being nice to inspectors. Besides, his nails were clean. An ominous sign.

I made a point of leaving my boots outside the door, as if that was my usual practice. True enough except when the phone rings and I throw caution to the wind. I scrubbed my hands as if preparing for a major operation and then put on another kettle of water for more tea. The occasion called for a feast of caramel slices. The pâté seemed to have disappeared without any ill effects.

He sat at the table and opened the briefcase. Gone were the days when an inspection was just a friendly chat, an excuse for the deskbound civil servant to spend a day in the country, making sure the cow wasn't tied up in the kitchen or the pigs weren't nestling on the hearth. Now it was all Acts and forms and regulations dreamed up in a foreign city.

"Now, let me see," he said, like a surgeon examining the patient to see the best place to make an incision. "*Philippa's Pantry*, I take it. Good name. Good name. You've obviously got a grá for the marketing end of things. I'm here to make sure the produce sits well on the stomach of the consumer." He demolished an entire caramel slice in one bite. A gulper, not a taster. A side of lamb or a roast suckling pig wouldn't go amiss.

"It certainly sits well on the stomach of the consumer," I said, a trifle miffed. "I can't produce enough to meet the demand. Everyone wants food that hasn't been irradiated

61

or filled with preservatives or colourings or scraped off the bones of animals after all the decent meat has been sold."

"There's not a thing wrong with mechanically recovered meat if the operation is carried out under the strictest hygiene conditions, which is our job."

"Of course MRM is safe, but people think they're actually getting real meat when they buy hamburgers, not bone scrapings or lips or eyelids. 'One hundred per cent pure beef' can hide a multitude."

He shuffled the paper noisily and I had an idea I'd said a bit too much. The man knew he hadn't a moral leg to stand on. However, he went the way of all men and put on the male sneer.

"You must be one of the 'muck and mystery' brigade."

I smiled as sweetly as I could and tried desperately to do one of those relaxation exercises where you imagine yourself in a quiet little spot with the sun shining down and the birds twittering like mad. However, I couldn't escape the feeling that a monster lurked somewhere.

Like a policeman at the scene of a crime, the Inspector stood up, his notebook open.

"Take me to your Pantry," he said. I looked to see if there was a smile. Nothing but inscrutability.

He caressed the tiles like a farmer assessing the bone structure of an animal. Cupboards were opened and a finger run along the shelves.

"I'll take some samples with me if you would label them with the date and batch number."

I put them into a box and held it out to him.

"The fridge needs defrosting," he said, putting the box under his arm. "There is a cobweb underneath the preparation table. The walls should be cement-finished, not tiled. The soap should be the liquid variety, not solid."

Like an idiot, I rushed to the defence.

"Of course I'm still learning. *Philippa's Pantry* is only a fledgling business, barely two years old."

"All the more reason not to kill off the customer. 'Think global, act local', isn't that what you would say?" with that gleam in his eye again. Seamus Mulready's little peccadillos were as nothing compared to these prejudices. A spoiler and killjoy who delighted in seeing the other person wriggle.

He brought out a pipe from an inside pocket, cleaned the spent ash onto the floor and began to fill it from a purse of loose tobacco. So much for practising what you preach. I coughed as loudly as I could when he lit up and as unceremoniously as possible, opened the window. He glowered and blew billows of smoke.

The demise of *Philippa's Pantry* seemed certain, the certificate as far away as heaven.

"Good day for a bit of fishing, rid the canal of a few pike," he said gathering his papers into the briefcase and snapping it closed.

"As soon as we have your registration fee, we'll send on your certificate." He walked towards the car. "Oh, and, good luck with the pigs," he laughed as he climbed in.

There ought to be a law against selling worms to people like him.

After a week in close confinement, when the sight of me clutching a bucket caused a stampede, I led the three little pigs to their "home" by dribbling nuts as I went. The wind in their snouts caused them to be a bit giddy but a rattle of the bucket soon brought them to heel. They hadn't lost their appreciation of the important things in life.

I coaxed them through the gate in the electric fence and introduced them to their little hut, a half moon of corrugated iron, painted green with oat straw for bedding. The oldest girl sniffed around it and began to scratch herself on the edge for all she was worth. I could have sworn she had a satisfied grin. The other two set their snouts to the ground and began to tunnel like prisoners of war in a new camp.

My purpose in getting them was to clear an impenetrable wilderness of bracken, gorse and brambles. Into this matted mass I tossed buckets of field beans. They watched as their food disappeared into the undergrowth and then sudden realisation dawned and, like a wrecking crew, they began to plough. With a herd of pigs, burning or bulldozing is totally unnecessary and you get a tasty morsel at the end. But try telling that to anyone.

What I thought would take a month of Sundays to clear was trampled to a pulp within days. The steady rain of late October had helped to create a small pond out of what began as a wallow. At this rate, I would fast run out of wilderness.

All the books suggested rings in their nose, just to keep them mannerly and preserve some measure of control over their tunnelling. However, I decided it would not be done without a local anaesthetic. The vet agreed.

I contracted PJ to help catch them in return for a tin of caramel slices.

"Stick the food in front of their nose there and I'll catch them unawares."

Easier said than done. A pig hasn't any useful "handles" like wool or horns.

In the end, PJ rigged up a lasso arrangement which he hid behind the bucket and pulled forward when the animal's head was busy dining. The rope was then tied around their hind legs and tethered to the gate. PJ stayed with them while I waited for the vet and escorted him to the scene.

He looked from PJ to the three tied-up miseries and back again.

"We'll take the one with the most energy first."

This was a toss-up. I shrugged a shoulder at PJ and he pulled the first to hand.

I was unprepared for the squeals that followed. They were the most human cry I had ever heard. I couldn't stay and lied about "something cooking". In the kitchen, I turned on the stereo as loud as I could bear to drown out the memory.

"Anybody home?" managed to penetrate and I came to with the vet shouting in the kitchen for all he was worth.

There was a long, narrow cut down one cheek and dark stains on his dungarees.

"You'll want to clean up," I said, not daring to ask who had won the round.

He nodded and took the offered towel and soap.

"Is PJ with you?" I asked.

"Gone home to get rid of the smell of pig," he said accusingly. "Said something about *two* tins of caramel something-or-other."

I put the kettle on. Deep in the freezer, in a special box, I keep a week's supply of delicacies in case of radioactive rain or a heavy fall of snow. It looked as if my Viennese Slices were called for. The vet was silent. Not even the reassuring steam from freshly brewed tea reassured him. I took out my cheque book and placed it nonchalantly on the table. That did the trick.

"Quite a crew you have there, Miss Woodcock."

It was obviously going to be expensive.

"However, a sore nose should cool their ardour for a day or two anyway."

He gave me another of his accusing looks. Strange how people blame the owner if their animal is rude and nasty. I suppose it's not very sporting to blame the beast.

"Interesting animals," I said as heartily as I could.

"They say they pay the rent but in my experience they eat you out of house and home," he said, swallowing his tea and putting the large cheque into his pocket. He left without a word, leaving a considerable dent in my bank account.

When the noise of the car was a distant hum, I fetched my piggie bucket of kitchen scraps, included a Viennese Slice as a special treat for them after their dreadful ordeal, and ran to the paddock to see the damage. Twelve legs shot towards me and three little snouts looked at me hopefully. One had a hole and a trickle of blood where there should have been a ring, the other was minus a snout tip and ring. Only the smallest boasted any decoration. I wondered whether to search for the missing snout and ring. One heard so many stories of fingertips and severed ears being sown back on. However, I realised in time that the airlift of a pig for microsurgery would be low on most people's list of priorities. Two legs have contempt for four legs.

"The 'gangrene swine' the Bible calls them. Rightly so. I've handled a bull easier." PJ, looking freshly laundered, shouted from the safety of the fence. "Bejaysus, as soon as their bonhams is reared I'd get rid of them lassies. The only place for a pig is in a book."

"I'm surprised at you, PJ. Where do you think those tasty rashers you eat for breakfast come from?"

He came as close to the electric fence as sense would allow and looked at me in that odd way of his.

"I suppose the next thing will be sides of bacon creeping up the chimney, smoking away. Me granny always said the taste was something else." Thankfully the memory was cheering him up. PJ rallies very quickly. Like a pig at the shake of a bucket.

"They'd hack a lump off it and toss it into the pot on the crane with a bit of cabbage; a few dozen potatoes bursting through their skins, butter dripping off them. Sure them days is gone. You were born a century too late."

"A century ago it would be unheard of for a city slicker

like me to toss it all up and return to the wilds. Most people spent their energy trying to escape into the city. Now the flow is the other way. Not a stream exactly but a tiny trickle."

"Well, good luck to them is all I can say. They'll never make a penny," he said, kicking a tussock of grass.

"Maybe that's not what's important, PJ. Perhaps they're looking for something . . . "

Our deep philosophical discussion was interrupted by grunts and squeals. One of the pigs had found a tasty morsel in the ground and the others wanted a bite.

"Just like children," said PJ, "except more useful. Give me a shout whenever you're slitting their throats. I've a hankering for a bit of free-range pork."

I gathered my buckets to more squeals and snorts. Food seemed to be the only thing on a pig's mind. They have none of the finer feelings of goats.

"Oh, by the by," PJ bent dangerously over the fence towards me. "I fell into a bit of land up the back there. An old aunt of mine used to run a few sheep and milk a cow on it. Three nice big fields. I had me heart in me mouth when they were reading the will. You can never tell what's in an old woman's mind. They get notions. But she did the proper thing in the end."

The "proper thing" was always to leave the land in the family, so that the tribe would grow strong and powerful.

"What will you do with it, PJ?"

"I'll buy a few more cows and some sheep to get the premium. None of them lads for me," he nodded towards the pigs. "Forget the caramel slices. I'll have a side of pork instead."

I didn't say a word.

Emily had to be shown not so much how to look after the pigs when I was away in Bath but rather how not to let them land her on her back. I put a long tube of plastic on the part of the electric fence which had the feeding trough against it.

"Now Emily," I showed her, "when they see you coming over the brow of the hill there, they'll go crazy for their food. Keep the cotton wool in your ears and quick as you can, pour the bucket of nuts into their trough and then retire."

"But surely they like a bit of human contact?"

"That's just the point, Emily. That's what this piece of plastic is designed to avoid."

She didn't believe me. Too used to the gentility of Poppy and Nanny and the shyness of the sheep.

"Emily," I said as gently as I could, "the kind of human contact they seem to like is someone with food. If they murder in the process, it doesn't seem to bother them. They haven't our insight to connect tomorrow's dinner with a two-legged person who's alive and well. They're creatures of the moment."

"They sound a bit like Seamus."

"Emily! I never thought I'd hear you criticise your friends."

"I'm not, Philippa. I'm merely making an observation."

I made a mental note to remember that one.

I got the Greene's order ready the day before I left for Bath and delivered it. Her house is a delight. A rectangle of cut stone entered by a tiny portico with fluted Doric columns, restrained and stately. Giant stone swans, heads obsequiously bent, sit on either side of the doorway. Wisteria and pale pink roses clamber up the walls.

Gaye Greene, a stunning vision in flowing white muslin lined with pink silk, opened the door.

"Philippa! What a surprise!"

"I thought I'd bring your things. I'm going away shortly."

"Oh, what a shame! Still, perhaps you'll be back before the next meeting. They're no fun without you. Come in, come in, we're just about to have tea."

She led me to a room of cool greens and bright yellows with a red and gold Persian carpet.

"Make yourself comfortable here while I put all these delicacies safely away."

The smell of pink jasmine, cascading from a Chippendale whatnot, almost overwhelmed me. I was brought back to my aunt's house in Dublin, its smell of dry rot, roast beef and several tomcats. Auntie Tilly foolishly thought a few strategically placed jasmines would camouflage the stink.

On a pedestal table made from cherrywood with walnut inlay, tiny daffodils stood green against the brown, their yellow heads trying to burst through. Just like Mrs Greene, trying to find herself, to grow, enjoy.

"Let's go into the conservatory. The freesias are in bloom."

Not freesias, of all things. Jack's favourite flower, the flowers he first gave me the morning after we made love and continued to give me until he died. The ones I placed on his grave.

"If you don't mind, Mrs Greene. The smell of freesias gives me a headache."

"We'll just stay here then. Simple."

She poured the tea from a Spode teapot, painted with delicate flowers. A copy of an old design. Auntie Tilly had the original. The cats drank milk from its saucers.

"Have a tasty snaster – that's what Dunkie calls them. Apparently it means a tasty morsel somewhere between a biscuit and a cake that's designed to tempt the palate."

I chose a circle of almonds embedded in soft toffee with one side covered in chocolate. Luckily I have all my teeth. Auntie would have had a horrible battle with it, like the time her top and bottom set got embedded in a meringue at a christening.

After a second cup and some one-minute praisings of Percy and Dunkie, Gaye took me to the window for a glimpse of the stud.

"That's him in the greenhouse."

A hand waved from a riot of colour.

"The cineraria and polyanthus are incredible this year. All thanks to Dunkie. Percy's delighted with him too. They plan to grow marrows and have races with Dickie's ones. I know who'll win. Don't tell poor Emily."

"So, tell me, how it is going?" I asked invitingly.

"Just wonderful. I can't describe it. It's like having a birthday party every day." I busied myself with the teapot, hoping the hate didn't show.

"Thank you, Philippa," she said demurely, taking a freshly filled cup. "Dunkie is so, so thoughtful. I have never had so much consideration since my poor mother passed away, God rest her. Every day there's something, either a present or a treat or a surprise."

"How does The Boss take it?" I asked, like the bitch I can be. Jealousy, pure and simple.

"No matter what, Percy and I will never part."

Mmm.

"Well, of course, it's all hush-hush. You're the only person I've told. I wouldn't breathe a word of it to any living soul," she said earnestly.

Except that the whole world knows about it already. I said nothing, of course. There is enough pain in the world.

"Of course not, Mrs Greene, you can trust me."

"I knew I could, Philippa. And," she said in a tiny voice, "please call me Gaye. It's really Gabrielle. Percy calls me that, sometimes."

Almost as rotten as Philippa. Parents have a lot to answer for.

"How fascinating. I shall have to call you GG!"

She pulled back a bit from this. I could see she didn't think it such a good idea. People can be odd about their name.

"Well, Gaye," I smoothed, "I'm pleased you've found what you think you need."

I was pleased at the way I put it.

"He's a wonderful person. So mature for his age and so knowing. Of course he spent a lot of time in France."

Indeed. If it's sinful, it must be French. The nuns always intoned about the evils of the parked car and "French kissing". We could hardly wait. At least half a dozen of us went to Paris straight after our final exams. Poor Jessica O'Connor, however, was brought home in a pine box after a particularly demanding party in the Latin Quarter. She should have followed my example and got rid of the whole business on the Aran Islands.

When the teapot was empty, Gigi insisted on showing me her embroidery. All hearts and roses. I must admit she's quite clever with a needle. Then out came the photo album. These things should be burned. What a bore going through page after page of someone's out-of-focus, ill-composed family groups. All the ones of interesting people, like those who stepped on boats and were never heard of again or the ones who tried to rob a bank with a plastic gun and couldn't start the getaway car, are burned or torn up.

I suggested a walk in the garden. Flowers cheer me up. So colourful, so perfect. The rudbeckia were still at their vibrant best, dark, shining eyes like velvet buttons. The delphiniums were almost finished, one or two spires bravely carrying on. Golden rod glistened gold in the sun.

"Percy does most of it. I just pick the seeds from the catalogues. I'm a bit worried just now. He's planning to knock down the garden shed where it all happened," she whispered. "Come and see it," she beckoned.

We were in front of it now. A square, wooden shed, nicely draped in the feathery blossoms of Russian Vine.

"He came to plant some Macrocarpa and ended up sowing seeds of a different nature! We were just inside," she said, opening the creaking door, "when he told me how taken he was with me. I thought it was a sudden brainstorm he was having but no, after a cup of tea we found ourselves there, on top of those old rugs."

They seemed to be none the worse for wear. More than could be said for Gaye. Women are so gullible. They think it's all to do with love at first sight, when for men it's simply an itch in the groin. Too lazy to do it themselves.

"I threw caution to the wind. I've wanted a baby for so long. After ten years with Percy, there's not much hope any more. I blame his mother, always smacked him when she found him touching himself."

"Speaking of procreation, much as I'm enjoying myself, I had better get back to Nanny. She gets quite fussy when she's expecting."

I couldn't stand any more of it. Whether it was envy or disgust I didn't bother to work out. Even the spinning course in Bath seemed attractive. At least I would have a rest from shovelling food into the pigs.

Nothing equals the boat journey from Dublin to Holyhead. In the old days, on my trips to France, it was merely the first leg of my adventure. This time, there was merely Bath at the end of it and a necessary and now not much looked-forward-to course on spinning and dyeing. There was always Gerald only a stone's throw away, of course. I was still kicking myself for Aran. However, there was no sense in seeming too eager. Besides, I owed it to the sheep. No sense in having their fleeces eaten by moths. And of course, the carpets and miscellaneous items would come in useful at the country markets.

The boat was packed to the gills with returning emigrants, like late swallows rushing for cover. Pale teenage girls sat with their overweight, worried mothers crossing the water to get rid of the mistakes. Life would never be the same again. Tatty cardboard suitcases bursting at the seams lined the aisles in the restaurant. The queue for the duty-free was long even before the boat left port. Luckily I had brought a decent bottle of wine, just in case.

I retired to my Pullman seat to pour myself a medicinal glass. An old woman I met in Provence told me never to travel without wine and garlic. Garlic to keep away the unwelcome attentions of other travellers and wine to "keep the digestion in good order". So, in the Provençal manner, I rubbed a clove of garlic on the bread roll I'd baked that morning and dribbled it with olive oil. A child in the row in front of me seemed intrigued and was practically in my lap before her mother yelled, "Jacinta, ye little bitch, come back here before I give ye a clip on the ear."

The Dublin mother is such a charming person. The child seemed nonplussed, stayed where she was and began picking her nose.

"I think Mummy wants you," I suggested through clenched teeth. That did the trick.

Later the same woman put a large, over-rouged face close to mine:

"Did ye ever see anything like it," she pointed a few seats ahead.

"At it all bloody night. Why they didn't get a cabin and do it in private I don't know. The rest of us have to listen to the slurpin' and breedin'."

I stood up and saw what she meant. Two bodies were closely entwined. It was difficult to see what they were exactly, male or female.

"It must be the heat in here," I suggested.

"It's disgustin', that's what it is. I didn't pay to see filth like this."

"Maybe we'd better keep quiet about it or they'll ask us for money."

This put a stop to her complaints. She spent the remainder of the night giving me bull's looks and pulling the child back from paying me another visit.

It was bitingly cold when the boat docked. The train was delayed, so we were herded into tin sheds to wait as best we could. I had the last of the garlic bread and wine.

The train reached Bath by nine. Fortunately, the Wayside Inn Bed & Breakfast Establishment was near the railway station. There were notices everywhere about dirty shoes, flushing loos, hairs in the bath and sanitary towels. Obviously run by a bossy ex-schoolmistress. I wondered why she still bothered putting herself through all the agony of getting people to do what she wanted. But then, some people enjoy coming the heavy.

Breakfast was self-service, just like boarding school. I got rid of my bags and went to the counter.

"Come now, Miss Woodcock," she bellowed at me. "You may have half a grapefruit or cereal and either two rashers or sausages with your egg but not both. This isn't the Hilton!"

"I wasn't fooled for an instant, Miss Death."

"D'Eath, Miss Woody. Amazing the number of people who can't pronounce it properly. But of course you're Irish."

"Yes, indeed. But for a quirk of fate I might have been English. Fortunately, my mother made it to civilisation in time."

She put two slightly charred sausages on my plate. I felt like giving them back but I decided discretion was the better part of valour. Besides, the course began in half an hour's time. My arguments take hours.

I made it to the Holborne with minutes to spare, arriving in a lather of sweat. "Dilly" introduced herself as our "Learning Facilitator". "Teacher" is not politically correct. With her mass of white, curly hair falling into her eyes and down onto her collar, she wasn't a million miles away from being ovine. Eighty if she was a day.

The rest of the class were "craftspersons", beavering away in the back of beyond, living "alternatively" on carrots and nettle soup. Everyone was being so wonderfully polite and jolly and eager to learn and ever so ecologically-minded. My favourite was the one with the earring through her nose and the purple lipstick.

On second thoughts, perhaps I would phone Gerald. Just to say "hello".

Dilly produced an enormous fleece that looked as if it

came from the abominable snowman. But no.

"This 'ere is a Leicester Longwool fleece. A lovely, twisted wool that gives nice little tufts to the finished garment."

From behind a partition she produced another fleece. Jacob, like my own.

"This 'ere is from the biblical sheep, wily old Jacob's sheep. A very light fleece but decent wool that gives nice mixtures."

"I'll have to defend the old Jacob's, Dilly," I found my disembodied voice saying, like a mother defending her offspring. "The weight of the fleece depends on the genetic inheritance of the ewe combined with her plane of nutrition."

"Well, seeing as how I don't know much about planes and genes and such like, I just know what's afore me," she said a little red-faced.

I shrivelled into the wall but managed to get a smile from the one with the nose-ring. I made a note to buy her a coffee.

By lunchtime, Dilly was surrounded by a sea of white wool, having produced a fleece from every available breed of sheep the world over. I wondered if I might be better off selling my fleeces to one of these industrious folk rather than doing the job myself. It all seemed slightly tedious.

When the bell went, I made a beeline for the nose-job.

She stretched out an arm with broken fingernails embedded with grime. "Gloria," she said, shaking my hand like an apple tree at harvest-time. "Isn't it just so wholesome to be dealing with all that natural product, straight from an animal's back?"

I was afraid she might want an answer, so I just nodded.

"So much of our lives is out of a box or a packet," she continued. "We've become so contrived and manufactured."

I glanced at the ring in her nose.

"I'm hoping to give up my job in the Social Services Department and move with my boyfriend to the Mendips. We've just found a lovely little place, full of character. The roof needs a few slates and the floors are a bit damp but the view is spectacular."

Indeed. Will that sustain you through the long winter nights, with the rain pouring through the roof and down the walls, I was dying to ask. I nodded instead and wondered whether Gerald worked at home.

"There's a little orchard of cider apples. I got a terrific press last week at the open air market in Wells. In two year's time we should have barrels and barrels of cider."

So there would be something, at least, to numb the pain.

"Cider is wonderfully refreshing," I smiled.

Lunch was quite something. Big chunks of cheddar cheese with pickles, brown bread and ale. A second helping had to be paid for. I treated Gloria to another ale. At the rate she knocked it back it would take gallons of cider to make a dint in her consciousness.

"Does it have an engine – your cider press?" I enquired.

"Not exactly. It can be hitched up to the hydraulics of a tractor though or to a millwheel. Of course, we have neither of those – yet. But Hank is a mechanical genius."

A very tall, thin girl, an Addams Family lookalike, pulled up a chair without a by-your-leave. Tentacle fingers stretched for the mustard which she lavishly spread over the cheese. Meticulously she cut it into tiny slices with a penknife attached to her bracelet.

Anorexia, without a doubt. I had missed whatever Gloria was telling me about Hank and caught the tail end of something about eggs and how between these and the pigs they would be well able to make a living.

I could have told her about the cost of food and rat poison and trips to town to stop you going mad.

Anorexia cast a dreamy eye towards Gloria.

"Did it hurt?" Puzzlement.

"The nose-ring."

"Just my pocket. It was either that or a new pair of shoes. Hank made the shoes."

She pulled up her tie-dyed dress to reveal a hairy leg and what we used to call Jesus boots, a flat piece of leather through which thongs were pushed to form toe-pieces. Just the thing for gathering apples and feeding pigs.

"Cool," said Anorexia. I thought the word a bit passé but then, when the brain isn't getting any nourishment, it cannot update.

For some reason, I began to search my bag for Gerald's number. He could only say he was too busy and that would be fine. Perhaps it would be better to leave it until my last day. Then it wouldn't matter whether he didn't want to see me since I'd be going home anyway. Much worse to feel miserable and have to learn to spin into the bargain.

We left Anorexia to her collection of cheese pieces, which seemed to have multiplied, and made for the Holborne.

Dilly was in the throes of telling an enraptured audience about the esoteric dyes she uses to make the peculiar garments she's arrayed in.

"'Grunge' they call it," Gloria in Excelsis put a word on my unspoken thought. I'm sure there's a better title.

"This 'ere waistc't," Dilly went on, ignoring Gloria and me, "I wove on a simple little loom using ends of wool. Just knotted them all together," she smiled like a child pleased with a messy painting. Too sweet to be wholesome. Anorexia came in and sidled to the back and Dilly called us to attention.

"The fleece 'as to be oiled well. Some of 'em dry out something terrible and they won't spin. So rub the oil well in. I always use vegetable oil, 'cos it's 'ome grown. All them yellow flowers you see in the fields, girls, is rape. Makes a good oil. No sense in putting money into Mr Frenchman's pocket for his sunflower oil. It was 'im what gave us garlic, the scourge of cooking nowadays. Everywhere you go, you smell the rotten stuff. Like dirty socks."

"Keeps the vampires away though," I said with a little laugh. Silence. Not even Gloria moved. Dilly stared straight into my soul.

"Well, we ain't got no class of vampires in our country. Can't say the same for anywhere else!" She looked at the rest of the room and smiled.

"Now, girls, let's get on with it."

I decided to phone Gerald at the break.

The phone rang for ages. Probably about three times. And then the answering machine clicked in. I felt like saying something really rude but decided I had enough enemies to be going on with.

"Hello, Gerald. It's Philippa Woodcock. I'm in Bath attending a very uninteresting course, 'How to Become a Spinster'. Would welcome a break for a cup of coffee if you're interested."

I ran into Anorexia in the loo, probably taking her laxatives and getting rid of whatever she'd eaten. If only the girl looked happier about being anorexic. Like alcoholics. They all looked so miserable. Why not do something different, I wondered. Like put a ring in your nose or produce gallons of cider or be like me, full of the joys of winter.

The remainder of the afternoon was spent "teasing wool" – "How unkind," I remarked to no one in particular and caused a titter in the back of the class. Teacher was not pleased. She got her own back by muttering something about "vampires". At five-thirty, we left in single file. I tried to bid farewell to Dilly but she wouldn't listen. Some people have a habit of holding a grudge. No sense of humour.

Gloria and I retired to the nearest pub. She had a pint

of cider and I had a large brandy. The barman offered us pickles and shrivelled sausages which we devoured.

"I don't think I'm Dilly's favourite person today," I remarked between sips and chews.

"Perhaps a bit too independent for her class of person. She likes to be Queen Pin."

"She's welcome. I have no intention of fighting for a leadership contest. I have my own little dung heap at home."

"You're not married?" So, here it was, the enquiries, the comments, the advice, the judgments.

"Almost. Several times."

"I suppose two out of three marriages end up in court. That's why Hank and me don't plan anything legal. It's too expensive to get out of it. I already hate the way he scratches his bum when he's thinking. We don't know if we'll like each other forever and ever."

"I'd never have felt that way about Jack. He was the nicest person you could imagine. Considerate, charming, interesting. We loved each other. Never out of each other's sight. We worked together, sat in bars together. Chatted non-stop."

"What happened then?"

"He died."

My wonderful, perfect Jack died.

"Oh, God. I am sorry. I wouldn't have . . . "

"Don't worry. It was a while ago, though sometimes it feels like yesterday."

I suddenly didn't feel like finishing my drink.

"I must rush, Gloria. I'm expecting a phone call."

I prefer to cry alone.

I walked down Great Pulteney Street, through Laura Place and crossed the river at Argyle Street. The Avon looked dark and cold, rushing on to Stratford, an endless flow forever and ever. Nothing like water to still the mind.

It's so busy rushing on, relentlessly. Loneliness is a strange thing. It cannot be shared.

At the Wayside Inn the Grim Reaper had left a cold mutton pie and a stuffed tomato for me. She had gone out to play bridge and her aide-de-camp, an obsequious lady in pink taffeta and a blond wig, presided over the hapless guests. I sat and watched a re-run of *Casablanca* and felt the agony of separation as it came to a close. Oh joy, oh bliss.

Of course, I could always burn the fleeces I had accumulated.

As I nodded off to sleep I remembered I hadn't left a phone number for Gerald. Maybe it was all to the good.

Having mercilessly teased and oiled the wool, we graduated to hand carders. Only the adoring few at the top of the room were allowed to use the drum carder, while the rest of us scratched our wrists on metal hooks. The idea was to bring all the staples of the wool into alignment and produce "rolags".

Dilly left her throne and wandered around the back of the room to make sure we had the right idea. She squeezed her way past Gloria and sought me out. She even had a smile. I couldn't believe it. Perhaps she'd lit a candle for me on her way home last night.

"Not bad, not bad. A bit thick 'ere and a bit fat there. Never mind. You'll get the idea."

I nudged Gloria, who had decided to sit beside me from now on.

"A bit more civilised today."

"When I told her about your boyfriend, the one that died, she said, 'Poor dear'."

"You told her about my boyfriend!"

"Well, yes. She came into the pub when you'd gone. We had quite a nice chat. I didn't know it was a secret . . . "

Not exactly, but I don't want the whole world and old

biddies like Dilly to know anything about me. Pity is the worst thing of all. It makes people feel they're one up on you. But I said nothing.

"No. Of course it isn't."

I would just be careful what I tell you in future. Maybe Anorexia isn't too bad after all. She seems to keep herself to herself.

By the time lunch arrived, I had a stack of rolags that would have choked an elephant. Perhaps Emily would like to learn to spin. I could supply the wool.

Dilly gave me a disgustingly fulsome smile as I left the room.

At the end of the corridor, silhouetted against the bright doorway, was a figure I recognised. Gerald. I almost ran.

I put my arm through his and like an old married couple, we pushed our way through the doors and out into the crisp day. Gloria and Anorexia stared in dismay. As I turned to wave, Dilly brought up the rear, taking it all in.

"Where to?" Gerald asked.

"Anywhere. Anywhere at all."

The "Petit Paris" was not *le dernier cri* in French cuisine but it didn't matter. An open field is as welcome when the company is good.

I wondered how Gerald found me so easily.

"Us mystery writers are used to solving puzzles. What I had was Bath and a Spinning Course. It took two phone calls to work out where you were. More coffee?"

"No, thank you. I would like a brandy though. I should have made you work harder. Anything that comes easily is never appreciated."

"If you're talking about you, Philippa, I appreciate you very much."

"Don't be so nice to me. You've no idea what an awful character I am."

"I don't believe it for an instant."

The afternoon was a haze. There was a park and water and then a famous crescent of houses. Then it was suddenly dark and cold and a fireside beckoned.

"There's always a roaring fire at the Wayside Inn, if you'd like to sit and warm up," I suggested.

Mrs Terminal gushed at us at the door. Not trusting me, she introduced herself to Gerald.

"Mrs D'Eath. Will you be staying to tea?"

"If you're sure you can manage an extra slice of bacon," I said, pleased I'd got in my retaliation. She led Gerald to the fireside and gave me a dirty look as she passed.

Tired from teasing and oiling, I let myself down and promptly fell asleep. I was sure I snored my head off. I've a sneaky suspicion Gerald did the same. However, we simply smiled at each other and said nothing.

The tea gong sounded and we made for the dining-room with its heavy mahogany furniture and white damask tablecloths covered with clear plastic. Two little old ladies darted glances at us from the farthest corner. Presumably residents on a cheaper rate.

The lady in the pink taffeta served us. She didn't look at me but gave Gerald one of her smiles. I was glad I'd been spared. I have an aversion to ill-fitting false teeth.

Gerald's plate was decidedly bigger than mine, crammed with mushrooms, kidney, two eggs, fried bread and grilled tomato all nestling on a bed of thinly sliced gammon. Mine had one egg, a slice of bacon and a tomato.

"Like some?" Such a nice person.

"If they catch you they might happen to let something accidentally on purpose fall onto your jacket. Or perhaps rip the lining from your coat in the hall."

"Really, Philippa. You have a very jaundiced view of human nature."

Gerald is so naive. He has spent too much time in his

attic and failed to notice the rest of humanity.

He halved everything, watched by the little dears in the corner. Whispered messages were then relayed to the vision in pink taffeta. When the table came to be cleared, there were no smiles, no extra biscuits and the tea was allowed to remain cold.

"A fresh pot of tea, please," I said, taking no nonsense.

"I see what you mean, Philippa. It seems I have been consorting with the enemy and must now pay the price. Perhaps I should pull your hair and get cross with you."

"Then you'd find a large slice of chocolate gâteau and fresh, steaming tea before you. The watchers in the corner see everything."

"There's a good mystery story here somewhere."

"The biggest one is why such a nice man is with such an awful creature as me."

He smiled but didn't rush in to reassure me. Probably just as well, I wouldn't have believed him anyway. I was aching to know whether he was returning to London or whether he was staying overnight. I didn't want to seem as if I had a vested interest either way, so I let things take their course. Amazing how slowly time passes when you're wanting to know what's going to happen next. We retired to the fireside and the television. Half past eleven and no sign of Gerald making a move. It was my bedtime. If I was to have any energy to cope with Dilly and all the spinning I had missed, I had better get to bed.

"Well, Gerald, it's time I hit the sack, much though I'm enjoying your company."

"Good idea," was all he said.

That queer lurch in my tummy was back. Was he going to exit gracefully or make some demands?

"I've booked in too. I'm just down the corridor from you." I must have had on my puzzled look.

"I arranged it when you were having your beauty sleep. It seemed the sensible thing to do."

"Of course."

I had packed my best frillies at the last minute, probably because they're silk and very comfortable.

At number 46, Gerald took my key and opened the door. I felt like a sixteen-year-old, awkward and embarrassed as I stood around, wondering what next.

"Well, now that you're safely in port, I'll wish you goodnight and sweet dreams." And he was gone.

"A'course, those what missed yesterday's lesson, will just have to get on as best they can. Mustn't hold everyone else up." Teacher was cross with me.

"Never mind," Gloria whispered. "I'll show you."

The idea was to twiddle the spindle with your right hand and by judicious feeding of the thread of wool already attached to it, the rolag in the left hand became part of the thread. Simple, if it didn't break or go too quickly and get lumpy. There was no doubt in my mind that Emily would be very well cut out for this kind of thing. I would give her a present of a fleece and a spindle and show her the rolags.

Anorexia was flying at it. Those long, thin fingers were surprisingly dexterous – I suppose from long practice in chopping tiny morsels of food. In no time she had enough wool to make a tea cosy. However, it was a coat she was aiming for. The poor thing felt the cold.

"Cider is what you need," Gloria advised. "It's got some sort of minerals in it that help the blood vessels to cope with cold."

No doubt. I'm all in favour of home remedies. Perhaps I ought to try it.

"I must pay you a visit in your Garden of Eden, Gloria. A glass of cider would go down a treat on a hot summer's holiday."

"Oh, there'll be all sorts of goodies. Home-cured ham dangling from the chimney, being slowly smoked by oak shavings. Rows and rows of Kilner jars filled with the tiniest silverskin onions, baby cucumber, peaches plucked from the south-facing wall, apple slices and ginger and lots, lots more. In the evenings, when friends call I'll open a jar and a barrel of cider and there we'll sit in front of the warm fire, swapping yarns and planning next year's garden."

"Sounds just like *Little House on the Prairie*," Anorexia said, her eyes glazed.

That was the trouble, I felt. Total fantasy.

"I hate to bring in a note of realism, Gloria," I began gently, "but the fact is the only callers you're likely to have in the country are the people you knew in the city who come once to see how it's going for you. They'll come, they'll look – if you're lucky they'll lend a hand till they collapse from exhaustion at having to make any physical effort. And then they'll go home and say 'My God, aren't they mad! I'd rather have my rubbish collected, good roads and paths to my house and not have to spend my time bothering with animals and digging the garden.'"

"Oh, I think the country is beautiful," Anorexia said, her face almost animated. "I wouldn't mind about the dirt."

"Most people do. They want to pass from a clean house into a relatively clean office. They want to be protected from the smell of dung and muddy boots. What most people want is designer nature – the fresh air, but not too cold or wet, the taste of good, fresh food – but without the hard work and effort."

When I stopped, there was silence. Heads were turned towards me. Dilly had on a cross face.

"'At's the truest thing anyone ever spoke. 'Ah couldn't have said it better myself. Laziness, that's what it is. Not prepared to put in the time. How many of yous will continue spinning after you leave here, that's what I'd like to know!"

I didn't blink an eyelid.

Gerald stood leaning against one of the Holborne's Doric columns as we trailed from the building at lunchtime. He looked almost handsome in his long pale coat, the collar pulled up against the cold. I presumed he was there to meet me, so I marched up to him.

"I've to go back to London sooner than I thought. May I buy you a farewell lunch?"

I was cross with myself for feeling a little twinge of disappointment. What difference would it make anyway, I'm used to being on my own.

"Never known to refuse."

He looked at me.

"Lunch, I mean," I added hastily.

We walked through the gardens towards the centre of town. In York Street we found a medieval building with its timber frame still intact, now a restaurant boasting home-cooked everything and château-bottled wine.

"I insist on paying for the wine, Gerald."

"I wouldn't dream of arguing with you, Philippa."

All my favourites were on the menu – mussels in garlic butter, Dover sole and a huge array of vegetarian dishes. I suggested a bottle of Gros Plant for the fish, Mâcon Viré for the main course and a Barsac to finish. Gerald ordered champagne to begin with.

I've been around long enough to know there's no such thing as a free lunch. The man was obviously bent on seduction. Think positively.

"I've just sold a play. The price was better than I thought," he said as if he could read my thoughts.

"What is it about?"

"People. Mostly." He swallowed the glass of champagne

in one go. I did likewise in the belief that "mirroring" is a good way to allow the other person to feel you're "with them".

"You don't say!"

"I wasn't being facetious," he said as he refilled the glasses. "It's about two women discussing their mother."

"What an absolute bore!" It slipped out, the uncensored feeling.

"It interests me that you use that particular word. 'Bore' can mean so much. Perhaps, I respectfully venture to ask, an unwillingness to examine the mother/daughter thing?"

"Of course. What else! Do we have to examine the ugly ghosts that rise up from the mind's fermenting cauldron? All that sort of thing is best left alone. We have to get on with things. No point in raking up the past."

"For me that cauldron is full of the most exciting, interesting and extraordinary things. I get a lot of pleasure stirring it up."

"*Chacun à son gout*. I prefer to keep the manure on the compost heap where it belongs. I don't bring it into the living-room."

"You're assuming there is something unsavoury about the 'manure of the mind' -- if I may borrow your analogy. Don't forget, it decomposes to a beautiful, sweet-smelling, rich material that makes things grow."

The bubble suddenly went out of the champagne. I was dying for a cigarette but I'd given that aberration up long ago when I smoked my last Gitane, the day Jack was buried.

I ate the cannelloni with four cheeses in silence. I felt like crying into the tomato sauce for me, for Jack, for everyone. I restrained myself.

Gerald put down his fork and reached a hand towards me.

"It's difficult, this business of living."

I nodded and nodded again.

I decided to play hooky from school and give Dilly a miss in the afternoon. I had an idea as to how I would love to spend it. It included clean, white sheets. However, we made for the Roman Baths instead.

In the Pump Room, where poor Jane Austen probably spent many a weary hour, we had a glass of the magical water. Disgusting and undrinkable.

"Dickens said it tasted like 'flat-irons'. That was being kind," Gerald grimaced.

We went to admire the clever heating system in the baths, saw the sauna and spent a pleasant moment or two gazing at the soupy water steaming into the cold air.

"Amazing how the Romans found the only hot spring in the country," I was about to say when Gerald planted a kiss on my hand. I pressed it meaningfully to his lips and wished I could fulfil my fantasy. If only I had that opportunity in Aran once more.

We walked down Pierrepont Street towards Hyncombe Hill and the Wayside Inn. Perhaps there was hope. The bed was big enough. I had on all the gear. We could shower first. Together. Like that couple in France in the university showers who did so all the time. Except the noise was dreadful. Like elephants snorting. Water everywhere. They even brought a stool. My imagination ran riot with that little prop.

Our seat by the fire was taken by the two old dears, the watchers at the gate. Gerald glanced at me, as if about to say something and changed his mind. We walked upstairs. On the landing he hesitated.

"Philippa, I must go back to London. I have to leave as soon as possible."

I returned to my spindle feeling thoroughly disgruntled.

Dilly looked not only displeased but definitely cross.

"Some people come 'ere under false pretences. They claim to want to learn all about spinning and dyeing and such like but want nothing of the sort. Gadding about is all they want. Wimen!"

Would it have been excusable if Gerald had been a woman? Did Dilly have a *petit secret*?

"Dreadful, isn't it, Dilly. I'm afraid I'm a lost cause, a Mary Magdalene."

The others laughed like lunatics. I was so fed up, I was becoming reckless.

"I 'ope, I 'ope," poor old Dilly spluttered, "yer spindle breaks!"

"Well, I sincerely hope so too, Dilly, because I have no intention of spending one second on this mindless activity we've been engaged in all week. I'm sure it turns the brain to wool in the end."

You could have heard a pin drop at that. Peace at last. I sat at the back of the room. Gloria didn't look at me. Anorexia lifted her eyelids and dropped them as quickly. The girl with the callipers turned and smiled. At break time, she came and sat beside me.

"Better to be cross at her than take it out on yourself. These things," she said pointing at the leg irons, "make me so angry I could chop my legs off. But I chop other people's heads off instead. The worst time was when I fell at a concert, down the steps. I was so angry at myself for falling, so upset that I was flat on my face. So I screamed and yelled and told everyone to fuck off and leave me alone. I felt better then. By the way, Gladys is what I was christened. You can call me a cripple if you like, 'cos that's what I am."

Nothing like someone being honest about themselves.

"Very interesting course, don't you think?" I ventured. "A wonderful way to keep busy, take your mind off things."

"It's about the most boring thing I've ever done. Raking

gravel would be more interesting," she replied loudly enough to be heard.

Dilly was fiddling with a gas ring and a pot of water. Like a witch with her brew, she threw in some bits and pieces. The smell grew more and more foul, like the Liffey on a sunny day with the tide on the ebb.

"This is our last day, ladies. Some of yous will have enjoyed learning all about the ewe and her wool. A'course, some of yous will have found it boring," she said staring meaningfully in our direction, "but that can't be helped. We do our best."

God, the violins would be playing next. No doubt she'd go home and cry into her lentil burger. Several people in the front row turned and gave us dirty looks.

"Well, I think your course was terrific, Dilly," the one in the front row with the hair dyed off her head sugared. "My spindle will never be idle."

Thank goodness for that. At least it would keep her off the streets.

After interminable hours of mordants, wode, onion skins, twigs, the merits and demerits of washing the wool before or after dyeing, we were released.

Gladys and I crawled our way to our Ploughperson's lunch. The others were busy at the trough, Anorexia chasing a pickle around her plate and Gloria swilling back the cider. Getting in as much practice as possible, no doubt.

No one was for chatting much. Stupidly I began to think about yesterday's lunch and Gerald. I felt the note in my pocket he left for me. Unopened. That way I could imagine all the wonderful things I would like him to say and then all the opposite possibilities. Once these were exhausted, I would open the envelope.

I ordered us a bottle of wine to mark the end of our week. So important to acknowledge the end of things, otherwise there's a mountain of unfinished episodes we cart along with us.

After a glass, we were all quite amiable again. Another bottle was ordered, just to clear away the "taste of wool" someone said. One reason is as good as another.

After that, we exchanged addresses, telephone numbers and invitations. Always a silly thing to do. As soon as you go home, there's someone on the doorstep who "just happened to be passing". However, I was past worrying. I could always set the pigs on them, feign chickenpox.

Soon everyone had gone except me. And my note. I opened it.

> *My dear Philippa,*
>
> *There seems to be so much left unsaid and I would like to be honest and straightforward. Where to begin? Or, rather how? Perhaps we could spend some time . . .?*
>
> *Perhaps you feel the same – I'd like to hear from you.*
>
> *I had to leave quickly. It was impossible to stay any longer without . . . without saying more.*
>
> *Yours,*
> *Gerald*

Intriguing.

I took the route we had taken last night, over Pulteney Bridge, past the Guildhall, down Pierrepont Street touching the walls, remembering what we'd said on this particular spot, how we'd laughed just as we passed that doorway. But memories are never happy, the moments are gone after all, never to return. Even if we can duplicate the experience, it is never the same. The past is always loss.

I phoned Emily from the airport to tell her I was on my way and to see what shocks awaited my return.

"Philippa! Thank God! You must have heard my prayers."

"What's happened?" I shrieked, visions of rampaging pigs, Nanny caught in barbed wire, bleeding to death, Poppy's calf dying. I make a point of thinking of the worst scenario, then you get a nice surprise.

"Something dreadful. Awful. Some scum of the earth opened the polytunnel to the frost. Dickie's marrows are dead."

I couldn't wait to get home.

Emily was on the doorstep the following morning.

"He's still in a terrible state," she said between sips of my piping hot crème de cassis. An old family recipe. Two bottles of burgundy and two pounds of blackcurrants, strained and blended together. Delicious, though at 11 am a little early for indulging in. However, I made an exception for poor Emily.

"You should see them, lying about, exposing their insides as if some terrible disease had struck."

"There's nothing worse than death for making a mess, Emily."

She looked at me. "Who could have done it?"

I had my suspicions but didn't dare say a word.

"Not one of the children?"

"God, no. They're trained from the cradle to respect the marrows. I often said to Dickie the children would grow up thinking a marrow was God the way he carried on. And my mother is no longer with us, God have mercy on her soul. Anyway, here am I telling you all my woes and haven't asked you a thing about Bath."

"Nothing much to tell. I couldn't help thinking when I was there, how much you would appreciate the craft of spinning. Such an old one and so simple. And now that I have the expertise, not to mention the wool, you may be interested to see how it's done."

"I'm just mad about crafts. I've just finished a tea-cosy

for Dickie's mother. Mauve and white because she's superstitious about green. She has her little quirks. I often wonder what Dickie's father was like. Every time I ask her, she just says 'Oh, that was a long time ago.' Dickie's too attached to her, worries about her all the time. That's why I had to knit the tea-cosy. She told him her tea was cold by the time she'd finished the first cup."

"Perhaps she could help out with the spinning too. Teasing, for instance."

"She's not really able for anything, though when it's time for a nightcap, she's truffling away for glasses, boiling water, the whiskey, lemon – all the gear. Not a bother on her."

I had all the spinning instructions, wool, carder and spindle in a little box.

"This," I said to Emily, "is all you need to know about spinning. Take it home, digest it and come back to me if you've a problem."

"Are you sure, Philippa? Don't let me take advantage of your good nature, after all, you paid a fortune for the course and here's me getting the benefit."

I wished she'd go before I felt guilty. The phone rang.

"Hello." Clara.

"Anything new?" I asked.

"I was going to ask you the same thing. See anything you liked more than yourself in Bath?"

No such thing as privacy. Once one person knows your business, the whole world knows within the hour.

"It's a wonderful city. The Pump Room has tremendous atmosphere and, what may be of particular interest to you, Clara, it has very medicinal waters, guaranteed to cure anything."

"And who were you sipping these waters with now, Philly? What were the men like?"

"Same as in any other city, unfortunately. Hairy, coarse and stank of BO."

95

I could see that Emily was horrified. I was a little surprised at myself but then it was a bit early to be tippling.

"But don't take my word for it, Clara. Have a go yourself. There's a hotel I can recommend."

The Wayside is just the sort of place to suit her. However, she wasn't interested.

"Speaking of recommendations, I hear a previous acquaintance of yours is to grace our humble Society with his presence."

"Yes. Eddie's a very nice person." He's a man, that's all that mattered to Clara.

We said our goodbyes as cheerfully as we could and I replenished the glasses. Emily was busy examining my doll's house.

"Poor Clara. I think she's given up on capturing a doctor. She says they all want to go back home and Pakistan doesn't appeal to her. All those bugs and spicy food."

Still silence from Emily.

"You would think she'd find someone. I'm sure she's very capable." Capable of anything I thought, leafing through *Farming News*. Emily had really clammed up. I was beginning to feel a little edgy, thinking of all the things I should be doing instead of sitting around, swilling crème de cassis. There were Kilner jars to be sealed and labelled, Nanny to be fed and her bedding changed, not to mention seeing whether Agatha was dead or alive.

"You know, Philippa," she said at last. "I hate marrows. I just hate them. Can you understand that? After all these years, I never thought I'd say such a thing. He has me as bad as the children, thinking they're the only things that matter."

I was glad I hadn't given her my best Waterford glass. I felt as if a volcano was about to erupt.

"They're only marrows, Emily. Silly old veggies," I said, oiling away.

"That's all they are, sure. But what do they mean to Dickie? They seem to be more important than the rest of us!"

Poor Emily was beginning to see the light. The truth is so painful.

I sat for hours when she'd gone, trying to get my bearings. I felt as though I had been away for an age, the house didn't seem at all familiar; like putting on an old coat that hasn't been worn for a while, you forget the way it feels.

I began with the Kilner jars, filled them with silverskin onions and put them in the pan. I prefer to use white wine vinegar, which is less harsh although the experts all say they won't keep unless the vinegar is strong enough to burn the roof off your mouth. Mine never last longer than Christmas. They and the pickled cucumbers are favourites at my annual party.

The fruit jar was almost filled. It was layered with raspberries, red, white and blackcurrants, strawberries, blackberries and I cheated with a few French cherries. The whole lot was steeped in brandy to preserve them. A Rumtopf, the Germans called it. "Heavenly" was my name for it.

The last of the apples had to be picked and put on the wooden slats in the store. They kept beautifully until spring, unless of course some uninvited scrounger happened to smell them out. I often found Nanny sniffing around the door frame, tormenting herself with the delicious apple aroma on the other side. Fortunately, she hadn't yet learnt how to undo bolts.

The butcher had murdered the lambs in my absence and they were safely tucked into the freezer. Poppy's two-year-old calf was still a bit on the lean side and would probably be ready in the spring. Which meant feeding the brute all winter. An expensive undertaking. Animals never stop eating for any length of time, it's not a case of breakfast, dinner and tea with little snacks in between. It's a banquet for twenty-four hours. However, at least I didn't have to rear a pedigree bull like PJ. He got through about a cwt of nuts and a bale of hay a day. More expensive to keep than a person.

It hadn't stopped raining since I got back from Bath. The ground was soft as a sponge, ready to gobble a wellington, the trees grey against a tortured-looking sky with big rain-clouds billowing from the west. The only cheerful sight was the last few apples, shining like lanterns on the bare branches. I climbed the ladder and eased them from their twigs. Nanny spotted me and came trotting over. I pretended one fell and it was finders keepers. If she thought for a minute I was the source, she would eat nothing until I "tempted" her with a tasty sliced apple. The trouble with Nanny is she thinks she's a person.

Agatha phoned. She was on top of her form. For a horrible minute I thought her cheerfulness was gin-induced, but no. She was actually pleased with life, for once. She even asked me how I was. I didn't tell her the whole truth. I wanted to avoid giving her permission to tell me how much worse off she was than me.

"I've great news. There's been a meeting with the doctors and they think perhaps I'd benefit from ECT. It has been known to cure depression."

"Electric shock, Agatha, surely that went out with the ark?" I said, horrified.

"Shows how much you know. It's still used extensively. In a certain number of cases it's been known to work wonders. Someone here had it last week and she was discharged yesterday."

"Yes, Agatha, but was her brain still intact? Perhaps it was still sticking to the electrodes."

"What a horrible thought, Pips. But as Mummy always

said, you are an eternal pessimist. It was always you who
spotted the sewerage pipe on the beaches."

"I see myself as a realist, Agatha. The only thing that
will help you is your firm commitment to quit the gin.
There is no easy answer. ECT won't do it for you, unless
you want your brain rewired. I wouldn't like that to happen
to you. It would be safer to give up the booze."

"You just don't understand what it's like to be depressed,
to feel nothing is worth doing, that it'll all be the same a
hundred years from now. And my business is going to the
hounds. I lost a contract today. The louse said he just
couldn't wait the few days it would take me to pull myself
together."

Weeks more like it. Poor Aggie. There are none so
blind as those who don't wish to see. Instead of the nice
bottle of Château Charenton-le-Puy I had put by for
dinner, I had a few glasses of spring water. Agatha would
put you off drink for life, or at least until tomorrow.

Dearest, dearest Gerald,

*How I wish I was back in Bath, wandering through the
steaming baths or even sitting with you in the Wayward Inn
(!) having a cup of tea and a ginger nut. My pleasures are
simple ones. I want Agatha to live. She has just been on the
phone, one of those calls which make it seem like an
instrument of torture. Instead of packing in the booze, she's
decided to have her brain electrically scrambled. God knows
it can't take much more beating. I feel so helpless and
useless. Everything I say is misconstrued – I'm supposed to
be the lucky one and she's the poor victim whom life has
treated badly. My toe itches to give her a good sound boot in
the backside but I know she'd love that. So, I'm left with
building up acid, getting a stomach like a ripe Gruyère. I bet
the doctors can't wait to hook up the electrodes. And they
call this torture "medicine"!*

As if that weren't bad enough, Emily's Dickie has forsaken marrows and is now embracing giant onions. The poor girl is beginning to realise what's been going on all these years. Perhaps I ought to encourage her to give them a little drink of some tasty herbicide. However, I've a feeling that won't solve her problem either. He just might take a liking to giant pandas instead.

Is there anybody sane out there?

Philippa.

I dropped my *cri de coeur* into the drawer of my bedside table to join the rest of the stack never to be posted. No point in letting Gerald know how things were. He thinks I have a grip on myself.

To cheer myself up, I set about organising my Christmas party. It's really a marketing exercise, when I display all that is superior and delicious in the Woodcock Pantry – in fact my labels say *Philippa's Pantry*. I even answer the phone with "PP Limited", or at least I used to, until Seamus and that episode beside Lough Gur. Him and his "Pippin" or "Golden Delicious" or whatever it was!

The delis phone me up and say, "Two dozen Philippa's Duck Liver Pâté, three dozen mayonnaise and half a dozen free-range ducks, stuffed." The latter was an inspiration on my part. Everyone is so fed up with chicken and stuffed, boned duck is out of this world. It involves removing every bone and filling it up with apricot, walnut and onion stuffing. Everyone goes mad for it. Even if someone rubbed my palm with gold, I wouldn't divulge the recipe.

For every one person invited to the party, there are six other people they tell about the delicacies of *Philippa's Pantry*. Several dozen orders for potted pâté would keep me going like the clappers all through Christmas, a lonely old time of year. I always think of the people who are dead, especially Jack, and I nearly go mad. I haven't really let go of him.

I wrote the invitations in my best calligraphy, using the picture part of last year's Christmas cards. I learnt calligraphy in Aix from a Chinese student who exchanged his teaching for English lessons. It was a nightmare. He laughed at everything, including me.

I dithered over Seamus's card. And Percy Greene's. I decided to address the cards to Noreen and Gaye. If they wish to bring their respective spouses, so be it. Dickie I don't mind. He's got his problems. As long as they don't go past onions and marrows, we're safe enough. If I get chatting to Eddie at the next meeting, I might just slip an invite to him. Of course, Gerald won't be able to come, but out of politeness, I sent him one too.

The rain hadn't let up outside, turning the paths to slime. The pigs hung about, looking forlorn. I almost felt sorry for them and boiled them a gigantic pot of potatoes which disappeared in seconds. Nanny walked as gingerly as an angel dancing on the head of a pin to avoid having mud creep between her toes. She's often at the back door in the mornings, rubbing her head on the window-sill. I wish I could invite her in for a cup of tea and a chat. She's probably more interesting than many's the one who's sat in the kitchen. Like PJ, for instance.

"What do ye want with goats for?" he asked me in that angry way of his. "They say they've the devil's soul, all sly and cunning," he said.

"Nanny has anything but the devil's soul, PJ." Not like some people I could mention. "Not at all sly. She's very clear in her demands." If only the rest of the world were as honest. But PJ is a cattle man at heart. All other animals are merely time-wasters, toys.

"For the cost of feeding that goat you could rear a nice calf and give yourself a few pounds. Calves aren't doing too bad now."

"Apart from the fact that you're buying in someone

else's bugs and the poor animal may not last a week, a calf wouldn't have Nanny's personality."

I knew this would inflame the farmer-businessman in him. I'm sure, at the end of the day, I make more money than PJ, who seems to chase rainbows and live on subsidy cheques. There are at least three people between him and the consumer of his beef, all making a profit, putting up the price of the finished animal so that the housewife finds it too costly to buy.

Judging by the look of sadness on PJ's face, he probably knew this without having it spelt out. What was the answer? It was the only life he knew.

"Thank you for your invitation, Philippa." It was Gaye Green on the phone. "Would it be okay if I bring Dunkie?"

"Of course," I replied, hoping that would be okay with Percy. She was obviously hiding nothing.

"It's just that he's almost part of the family now. He's moved into the shed permanently. Made a lovely log cabin of it. Wooden panelling and a wood-burning stove. I made chintz curtains and cushion covers to match. I had a test done and it's positive."

This was exciting. A million questions came into my head. I was unable to form one of them.

"We're all very happy about it. Dunkie talked about an abortion but Percy and I wouldn't hear of it. So now we're thrilled. Percy and I lie in bed half the night talking about it, wondering what we'll call it, what it will look like."

How cosy! And the father of it all in the tool-shed, appropriately enough. I was trying to take one breath at a time.

"Duncan is between jobs, so he's around to help me get things ready. We're just putting the last of the teddy bear paper in the little bedroom. A bit twee, but I couldn't resist it."

"I'm sure it's lovely, Gaye," was all I could muster.

"I've got a terrible craving for pâté, Philippa. Any chance of you being able to drop some in to me? I want to eat nothing but the best."

What a nice person Gaye is, her compliments are always truthful.

"I'll come as soon as I can. I've just made some wholemeal scones; we may as well make pigs of ourselves!"

I could always do the catering for the christening, I thought as I climbed into the car. One of those iced cakes with a tiny baby lying asleep under a quilt of white icing would go down very well. By the time I arrived at the Greenes', I had everything planned except the brand of champagne. I wondered whether they would stretch to the real thing.

"The baby's expected in July," Gaye said in her breathless way. "I feel great apart from a bit queasy in the mornings. But Percy gets me some hot apple juice and I'm right as rain after it. As soon as he's gone to work, Dunkie comes in and we have another cup and some biscuits, if I'm feeling up to it. So far, so good. But I've to take things easy. I'm not in the first flush of youth. So I spend a lot of the afternoon lying on the couch. Sometimes Dunkie reads some poetry, Wordsworth usually – though not the Lucy poems, they're too sad. And then he gets dinner ready. He used to work in McDonald's, so he has a fair idea of cooking. His mother was a *cordon bleu*."

"How nice for all of you. A *maison à trois*. Used to be very fashionable when I was in Aix."

Though it never appealed to me. All that arguing about who drank whose decaf and who left the tide marks on the bath.

"I brought you the pâté, only just made. I'll pop the scones in the oven and put the kettle on."

"You're a pet, a real friend."

I felt such a heel. I didn't feel like anybody's friend. I wasn't even sure what that meant.

The kitchen was immaculate. The pine was scrubbed white and smelt of beeswax and lavender. The door opened. Dunkie, I presumed.

"Hello," I said, stretching my hand in greeting. "Philippa. We waved at each other through the greenhouse last time I was here."

"Sure. Heard a lot about you."

Not another one. I wish people would say exactly what they heard or what they thought when they heard whatever it was. I suppose I'm better off not knowing.

"Gaye's just putting her feet up while I do the tea. Care for a scone?"

"Would I just! It takes a lot of energy to keep warm in that shack. Perhaps after the event, when they find it has only one head, I'll be promoted to the spare bedroom."

Sooner than you think, my boy. Someone will have to get up in the middle of the night. Breast-feeding might be a bit tricky though.

I brought Gaye a steaming scone filled with melting butter and pâté. I don't know whether she was more ecstatic about this or about seeing Dunkie.

"Hi, beautiful. How's little what's-his-teeth?" he asked, patting Gaye on the tummy.

"Swimming like a little fish in mummy's goldfish bowl. Very keen on duck pâté."

"So long as he doesn't get webbed feet."

A cloud crossed Gaye's eyes. A mother's anxiety over the normality of the little offspring.

"We're going to have a scan. Just to make sure everything's okay."

We were silent after that. There are no guarantees in this life.

I cleared away the crumbs and refilled the teacups. The

china cheered me up. Material things may be mere fripperies but yet they were durable, touchable, reassuring when life seemed insubstantial, evanescent.

As we passed down the garden path, through the now faded, final flush of roses on the archway, Gaye whispered, "Philippa, I'd be grateful if you would keep Dunkie and all that, you know . . .?" she said, patting her tummy.

"Of course. He's merely Percy's friend from school, between jobs, as we agreed."

Nothing would give me more pleasure. Although a secret is often burdensome, like a Sticky Willy we want to peel off. But I knew Gerald wouldn't tell a soul.

A card from Gerald when I got back, along with a substantial ESB bill. I really would have to stop reading in bed. There was certainly no way Nanny could do without her infra-red heater at night, now that she was near her time.

I poured myself a small glass of white wine, made some crisps with sea-salt and sat down to savour the card. Postmarked Paris. Indeed!

Dear P,

Staying on the top floor of a rickety old hotel close to Eiffel T. Reeks of garlic and cheap perfume. Shudder to think who's behind the closed doors! Wish it was you and me. They're going to publish Death of a Lover *in French. See you, G.*

No mention of when he was returning. I was torn between wanting to know his every move and not wishing to know anything. There seems to be a narrow line between creating an obsession and being indifferent. One had all the pain while the other lacked any pleasure. No sense in wishing things were otherwise. Work is always a good antidote to self-absorption.

I cleaned out Nanny's stall in preparation for her delivery. She had that absent-minded look about her, as if something is happening and she's not sure what it is. Her udder was filling up and her tail was high. I cut her ration slightly, to ease the delivery. She doesn't realise it's easier to give birth on an empty stomach. I filled her trough with rainwater; animals prefer its sweetness. Tap water is bitter, even if from a well.

I locked up, had a look at Poppy and her calf to make sure they were okay and peeped into Nanny's stall to see how it was going. Still no further forward. The sheep had already settled for the night, their humped shapes shining in the fading light. For once the pigs were still, lying on top of each other, their bodies shuddering with snores. Tonight was Eddie's talk to the Archaeological Society. My blue silk blouse was freshly ironed. I brought some honey to remind him of old times. He used to dab it in the most interesting places but it made a terrible mess of the sheets.

I cycled to Eddie's lecture. If I decided to take a lift, I could always play the damsel in distress and put my bike in the back of his car. Unfortunately there would be competition. Clara would have on her best bib and tucker, although surely she wouldn't stoop to her décolleté black number in the middle of winter.

The town was lined with cars. Not all for Eddie. The star attraction was a ventriloquist whose dummy did a striptease act, complete with commentary. I'm told it has to be seen to be believed.

They actually swept the floor of the pub for the occasion and put Eddie and his screen in a corner. Clara had obviously got there early, her large bosom busily caressing Eddie's box of slides. Seamus was sitting close to her, an untouched pint by his side, scrutinising each dimple and swell of pink flesh.

Noreen gave me a wink from the side of the bar.

"Some people don't worry about the damage a frosty night can do to their bits and pieces," she whispered deliberately loudly, her eyes flashing to Clara's cleavage.

"Don't worry your head, Noreen," I soothed, "they're probably silicone. The freezing point is very low. Although I have heard you mustn't sit too near a radiator."

"Can't you just see it – Christ, George, I'm on fire! I've heard of 'hot pants' in me day but never . . . "

Noreen tried to choke back the laughter.

I turned to see the interruption. Eddie, a smile as wide as a melon on his face. His teeth were still perfect. The things those teeth have chewed in their time.

"Pippy!" He rushed towards me. "How are you? Clara's been telling me you've been away since I saw you."

"You make it sound like the House of Correction, Eddie. I've been busy researching ways of disposing of my wool pile in the barn. A friend of mine is presently learning how to spin. All we need is a weaver."

"Get Seamus to volunteer for that job," Noreen said. "He's a great little weaver when he has a few drinks on him."

Noreen can get a little tiresome, given any encouragement. Eddie laughed out of politeness. Clara came to see what the jollity was about. She put her pearly false nails on his arm.

"We mustn't take advantage of you, Edward, and have you going home all that way in the dead of night. We'd better begin."

Eddie shrugged at me and allowed himself to be mauled by the tigress of Ballinamore. There was a rush for the bar as everyone got their supplies for the hour ahead. We shuffled to our places and the room was plunged into darkness, except for the halo of light around Clara, presiding over the box of slides. Silence. Seamus cleared his throat and spat on the floor. Emily sat on one side of me and Noreen on the other.

Eddie's disembodied voice caressed us from the screen in the corner. The slides were blurs of grey stones, withered grass, skeletons of our ancestors found crouched in the sides of eskers.

"That's definitely one of Seamus's forebears. I'd know that grin anywhere," Noreen nudged. I presumed she was joking and laughed. Clara's bosom gave an admonishing wiggle and she delayed the next slide just long enough to make me feel guilty. I'm afraid it emboldened me. I began to pay more attention.

"Eddie, if you don't mind," I intruded gently.

"Of course not, Pippy." I really must speak to him about calling me that.

"I was just thinking, how would we like to be on display for all and sundry in another few hundred years, with people seeing how our flesh had fallen from our bones, how many teeth we had?"

He looked back at the skeleton.

"For goodness sake, we're all the same underneath the skin," Clara said, clicking to the next slide.

So true, Clara. It's the bits on the outside that really tell us apart.

The door opened a crack.

"Sorry we're late." Gaye and Percy Greene with Dunkie in tow. They sat at the back and whispered.

"To answer your question, Pippy," Eddie continued, "it's really a moral one and ranks alongside the issue of preserving human parts in ether, like the victims of the holocaust or the tribesmen of New Guinea whose ancestors' heads sit in glass cases in the British Museum. I take your point. Perhaps I ought to leave a blank space where old skelly is."

"Well, I think we should have a minute's silence in his honour," Seamus slurred.

"Maybe we should have a bit of a break," Emily suggested. "Would that be all right with you, Professor?"

Eddie put down his pointer in defeat. Before I could stop myself, I ran to rescue him from deep depression.

"I was really was only a tiny bit serious in my question, Eddie. I didn't expect you to take it so literally."

"But it is serious, Pippy. Very serious. And I never thought of it before. Here's me exploiting a skeleton who has no choice in the matter. Come to think of it, I wouldn't like a group of people ogling at me, when I thought I was dead and buried and safe from harm."

The man was about to have a nervous breakdown. This was all I needed.

"Let me get you a drink, Eddie. How about something hot? Port and brandy?"

"I mean, when I think of the number of times I've shown that slide not to mention the half-dozen others I have. Poor Cro-Magnon man. Who's going to stand up for him? And what about all those foetuses, whose photographs are handed around like confetti. Is there to be no respect for them, not allowed to die in peace? Then there's the slices of cancerous lung showing the effects of smoking that are thrust into teenagers' faces. The list is endless . . . "

I thought of the animals in the zoo, caged and bored and stared at, of those in the museum, even tiny baby ones, killed in order to be stuffed. The evening was deteriorating rapidly.

"Well, Eddie, I'll get us both a nice drink and we can chat about old times."

Teresa and Dotty were at the bar, eyeball to eyeball.

"Evening, girls. Wonderful speaker, isn't he?" I said to both.

"Marvellous," said one. "Brilliant," said the other. Scintillating company.

Gaye, Percy and Duncan were tête-à-tête, a world unto

themselves. Gaye was drinking orange juice. At least the child would be born sober.

"Here we are, Eddie," I said, handing him a hot port and brandy. "That should banish all those silly worries." I ignored Clara who had placed herself next to Eddie, the tips of her breast brushing his sleeve. Seamus still had his eyes pinned to her.

I beckoned to Noreen to join us with her glass of lemonade.

"I've never understood men's obsession with breasts," I whispered to her. "They seem to see them as their playthings for their exclusive use. Forgotten is their prime purpose of feeding a baby."

"It was a man, after all, who invented powdered baby milk," Noreen said.

"Jealous his toy was being used by someone else. No doubt the psychologists would say it was lack of proper nurturing. Little buggers weaned too early, still can't get enough of it."

"It's this business about size and shape that pisses me off," Noreen said, pulling her cardigan across her ample chest.

We gazed in fascination as Clara attempted breast seduction with Eddie. She was barking up the wrong tree. Eddie is a leg man.

I drained my glass and turned to give it to Christy behind the bar. In the few seconds I had been away, the group had closed in on the gap I'd created. Eddie, Clara, Noreen and now Seamus, up to ogle at closer quarters, were huddled together. As if I didn't count, my presence dispensable. Like spotting the sewer pipe on the beach, as Agatha always says, I saw the faults and failings all around me. Gaye and Dickie and now Duncan brought into the fray. Seamus mentally massaging Clara; Eddie delighted with an audience, even if it is Clara. Noreen, disillusioned and slightly bitter. I decided to leave. Nanny probably needed me more.

It was bitingly cold outside. The road glistened like lip-gloss as I climbed on the bicycle. There was no need to say goodbye. I suppose some corner of me had hoped to chat to Eddie and talk about old times.

As I turned into the yard, there was no whimper of hello from Nanny's stall. The cat rubbed itself on my leg and I heard an apple fall from a branch I hadn't been able to reach. A welcome treat for Nanny when she had delivered.

I took the torch from inside the back door and went to see her. Not a sound. She surely would have heard me by now. I pulled the bolt and almost fell into the stall. There she was in the far corner, lying on her side. I ran to her. She gave a deep groan as she recognised me. I felt her nose and ears. Dry and cold. I looked at her tail end. Wet and swollen. No sign of a pair of legs. I rubbed her head. An eyelid flicked.

"What is it, Nanny? Baby not coming quickly? Maybe stuck. Hang on there till I get some soap and water."

I grabbed the rubber gloves, filled a bucket with water and put a slab of Sunlight soap into my pocket. I left the door of Nanny's stall open so that the light from the yard would reach inside. She looked even worse. Her neck was stretched even higher as if she was trying to escape from pain.

I knelt beside her and soaped my gloved hand. Gently, I put my fingers into her vagina. She groaned into the straw.

"I know, Nanny. It probably hurts like hell but I must get your baby out. Then you'll feel a whole lot better."

I found one foot. A head. The other foot was missing. Maybe turned underneath, holding up everything. If I could straighten it, then give both legs a little pull, we were in business. But no. Perhaps that wasn't a head at all. I pulled off the glove and felt again. But I was none the wiser. Nanny gave a little sigh.

"For God's sake, Nanny, don't give up. We'll get there."
Goats are great giver-uppers. They just lie down and take
what's coming.

"Come on, Nanny. I've a lovely juicy apple for you
when it's all over and a big dish of corn and barley, not to
mention some of that tasty hay you were trying to pinch
the other day. We'll have a nice big feed, lots of sweet
rainwater and your little baby to keep you company."

She wasn't listening. A Caesarean was the only answer.
A sharp knife, whip out the kid and clamp the skin
together until the vet came. Another groan. She must have
heard me. I put my hand in again. Definitely a mouth with
teeth. Good. We were getting places. Now for the leg. I
eased the head back slightly with my knuckles and whisked
out the bent leg with my fingers. With any luck I wouldn't
break it. So, two legs and a head. A pull on the legs should
do the trick. Nanny's body gave a gigantic convulsion. A
collection of legs and heads popped out.

"Nanny, you've got twins!" I shouted. They lay in a
heap, covered in placenta.

"Don't worry, I'll attend to them, Nanny. You take a
rest." Within minutes they were trying to put their long
skinny legs under them to stand up, sneezing and shaking
their heads.

"They're up now, Nanny. Like two drunks, barely able
to stand. Let me see, now. One is a boy and the other a girl.
One of each. A Protestant family."

I closed the stall door and switched on the infra-red
lamp to keep them warm. I turned round. There was
something about the way Nanny lay, so still, so sunken.

Not Nanny. Please, not Nanny. I knelt by her head. Her
beautiful hazel eyes stared at nothing in particular, past
caring about anything. Damn, damn, damn. Why? Oh why?

"So this is where you are!" Eddie.

"You sneaked off without a word! You missed hearing Seamus singing *The Mountains of Mourne Sweep Down to the Sea* as he eyed Clara's *décolleté*. Even I was embarrassed and, as you know, I'm not a prude."

He could have been anything. I wouldn't have noticed.

"Pips! Something wrong? You look awful."

I stood up and turned my back on lifeless Nanny.

"Is it dead? Must be a lot of money to lose."

"It's got nothing to do with money!" I shrieked.

I lifted a kid in each arm.

"Sorry. Can I do anything?"

"These two will need food and heat. Would you turn off the infra-red switch behind you?" Nanny wouldn't need it any more.

"I'll make us a cup of tea." Some small part of me was grateful for company.

The kitchen was cold. A tiny piece of turf glowed at the bottom of the range.

"Here, Pippy. You look after those two. I'll see to the fire."

"I wish to Christ you wouldn't call me that! Especially in front of other people." It just came out. To hell with it. I felt him tighten and hesitate with the bundle of sticks.

"Sorry, Pip, Philippa." I was relieved he conceded. I hadn't the energy for a battle.

"This goat of yours, she was very special?" he asked.

"Very. She loved me."

"Oh. I see," he said quietly and plugged in the kettle.

I had a tin of Florentines somewhere and some cheese puffs. I couldn't be bothered getting them.

"Had her long?"

"She was the first animal I bought. I picked her out from a whole herd of them on Gneevebawn. Her coat caught the light the way silk does, turning it almost to suede. She had such a haughty look. Snobby. And her big

113

nose and floppy ears. She followed me out of the field as if she'd been waiting for me all her life."

"She was just an animal, Philly."

"'Just an animal' as opposed to what – a human? Let me tell you something, Edward Henderson, Nanny had qualities about her that no human being could match. Ever."

Like her "hellos" whenever she saw me, completely sincere, untainted by what had gone before or what was to come. Skipping after me, watching every move I made in the garden and following me down to the stream to fetch water for the plants and back again. Lying beside me when we both had enough in the heat of the sun.

"I had a budgie once," Eddie muttered. "Blue with black spots. Had the most boring life imaginable, caged, eating the same old seed, swinging on the same old swing, wanking himself to sleep on the bars. Put me off animals for life."

I forced myself to get up and make tea.

"I'm sorry, Eddie. I'm not very good company. If you want to go, it's okay with me."

He rocked backwards and forwards in the rocking-chair.

"What a selfish asshole I am. Here's you going through a bad time and me thinking about a bloody bird."

"We're all entitled to our own thoughts, Eddie. There's no law that says we must put our own miseries second to someone else's."

I put the kids into the oven drawer on layers of newspapers.

"You know, Philly, I've often wondered why we never married."

I had a fair idea but for once I said nothing.

"Well, I took off to the south of France, if you remember, and you were busy with your PhD on Lough Gur," I said from inside the deep-freeze as I searched for milk.

"Yes. I remember now. You never let me know you'd returned."

"I hardly let a sinner know, Eddie. I had just buried my best friend."

"Buried?"

"Yes. You know, death."

"What happened?"

"Blood poisoning."

"He was injured?"

"Afraid so. I was into my woodworking phase, knocking up little olive wood boxes with brass inlays. I left some tacks lying about the floor. Jack stood on one and it festered and festered. He kept saying it was nothing. Even rushed him to Paris but it was too late to do anything."

"Was it serious – the relationship?"

"We were going to have a baby. Of course, we weren't married. That never mattered. Anything goes in France if you're an 'ètrangère'. They think you're mad anyway. Not sane and sensible like them."

"And the baby?"

"Died. At twelve weeks. I miscarried when Jack died. A tiny little thing with a big head and curved body. Perfect and yet not perfect enough. A girl. I brought her to the hospital in a coffee jar, hoping they could tell me what went wrong. They just looked and said 'Okay' and gave it back to me. I buried it in a flowerpot, under a fuschia, the flowers remind me of ballerinas. I couldn't bear thinking its life would be useless in the end."

"God, Philippa. I am sorry. You've had a rough time."

"Must soldier on. Onward, ever onward."

Poor Nanny. How would I bury her? I knew where. But how?

The kids began bleating.

"Little fellas a bit hungry. I'll make tea if you want to get some grub into them, Pips. Sorry. I mean, Philippa."

I emptied the frozen slab of milk into a pot. With the dosing syringe, I sucked up the melted liquid. The difficult bit would be getting the little brutes to let me open their mouths.

"They fairly clench those teeth of theirs," Eddie giggled.

"So would you if your head told you to expect a nice soft nipple and all you get is a lump of hard rubber. Trouble is, they're programmed to root out the nipple and will accept nothing else. They have to learn the connection between a full tummy and this thing in their mouth. Could be dead before they get the message."

"Who'd be a farmer?"

Some of the milk got in by the side of their mouth. Most of it trickled down their neck.

"See how the girl is more amenable. Got more sense than the silly male. It's the same with any animal. Males take an inordinately long time to learn."

Eddie was silent. He was no male chauvinist, if I remember rightly. One of the few men on the Condom Train to Belfast.

By the time the kids had a teaspoonful each of milk and their chins wiped, the tea was cold.

"Let's have something a little stronger," I suggested, getting the sloe poteen from the cupboard.

Eddie was kneeling down by the range, like a little boy, patting the kids, whispering to them. It was crystal clear why we had never married. There was a vulnerability to Eddie, a sort of innocence or naïveté which was a form of weakness, of regression. Not a strength, like an adult summoning up the child from within yet still remaining an adult. With Eddie it was a feeling that crept up unannounced, enveloped him in such a way that he became powerless. Endearing nonetheless. But definitely not made for the trials of matrimony.

After our second drink, I fed the kids again. No crackle

116

in their chest at any rate. Perhaps they would both survive. Eddie watched me intently.

"Philly, what about Nanny? I mean, the body of Nanny."

"Well, she's certainly not going to the hunt. I'll bury her in the morning."

"Just what I was thinking. Maybe you could do with someone who's a dab hand at digging."

No doubt weakened by the whiskey and Nanny's death, I nodded.

I made up a bed for him in the spare room, on the ground floor with a French window that led out to the front garden. A bleak scene at this time of year with the wet leaves lying like slugs across the grass. Empty seed-heads crackling in the wind. Summer's flowers, like Nanny, gone forever. It's always our own death we think of when someone dies.

When Eddie was settled with hot-water bottles and towels, I made myself a generous nightcap and went up to bed. No sooner was I nicely warmed than the phone rang. Probably Agatha with her brain hanging out after the shock treatment. I didn't feel up to hearing all about it, so I didn't bother getting up.

Seconds later I heard feet padding up the stairs. Eddie stuck his head around the door.

"Phone for you. A gentleman."

A species that is few and far between in my life. I felt distinctly woozy as I got up. I saw Eddie giving me an appraising look as I struggled into my dressing-gown. He could forget it. I wasn't in the mood and even if I were, I'm not sure I would want to relive my youth. I finally got to the phone.

"Hello. Perhaps it's a bad time."

Gerald!

"No, it's nothing of the kind. I'd just gone to bed."

117

"Hope I didn't interrupt anything. Just wondered how you were."

"Fine. Very well. Nanny died."

"Sorry to hear that. Was she a close relative?"

"My best friend – a four-legged one, of course."

"A dog is always a sad loss."

"She was a goat."

Silence.

"Well, just thought I'd say hello. Mustn't keep him waiting. Goodnight."

"Bye, Gerald," I said to an empty phone.

Eddie was standing at the bottom of the stairs. I could cheerfully have throttled him.

"Social life hectic these days?"

"It could have been!"

"Hope I didn't queer your pitch. If he's really serious, he'll ring back – just one more time, to check."

What Eddie knew about live tissue could be written on the head of a pin. Skeletons were his speciality.

I went back to my room and slammed the door. I didn't sleep a wink, what with every reel of Nanny's life being played in my head and remembering she was lying dead outside and then Gerald getting the hump on account of Eddie. It was all so unfair.

By six o'clock in the morning I'd had enough tossing and turning and got up. I put on my digging clothes, an old track suit I bought at the church sale, well fumigated and left on the line in the sun to kill any lingering creatures. The kids were still asleep, curled against each other, warm as toast. So far so good. I put on their bottle.

There was a most extraordinary noise coming from the spare room. I listened at the door.

"Hummmmmmmmmmmmmmm. Oinggggggggggggggg." Eddie doing some sort of mantra. Then the most dreadful pounding. His exercises! How sensible I was not to take his offer of marriage seriously. Heaven knows what I'd have had to put up with. I knocked on the door.

"Come in, Pips! How wonderful you look and so early in the morning. A flush to your cheeks."

Nothing to do with finding him stark naked.

"Morning is my best time," he said, coming towards me.

"Just wondered whether you'd like something to eat before we, em, do what is necessary for Nanny."

"Meat is what I like first thing in the morning. If live flesh isn't available, then a nice chop with some kidney, sausages and black pudding would do just as well."

"Ready in ten minutes," I said as I scarpered, pulling the door behind me. Men are most peculiar. They think the sight of a penis is enough to set a body on edge. Perhaps I ought to look out the machete Jack bought as a joke for me one birthday. Just in case. I really ought to see about getting a dog.

As soon as it was light, we got the spades and went into the orchard. In a corner, beneath the apple tree Nanny was so fond of, we began to dig. Eddie was fit as a fiddle and had the hole dug in no time.

"Time for the cadaver," he said, putting an arm around me. "It's really hard luck. Still, it's nice she's left her little offspring behind." He squeezed me tightly. I didn't mind a bit.

"That's one of the few things that gives life meaning. What we leave behind. Our mark. For most, it's children. My legacy will have to be something of what I've created here," I said looking around me. "I try to add to it all the time, give the soil proper nourishment not just mine it for all it's worth. I'm really only a caretaker. It's not mine for eternity."

"Pips, you're so, so wise. I've often thought about you, remembered things you said. I used to write them down. Did you know that? Stacks of 'Pippy said'."

"That frightens the wits out of me. I probably said the first thing that came into my head."

"I don't believe it." He stopped and looked at me. I felt my tummy tighten. Not this. Not now.

"In fact," he went on, his forehead crumpled in earnestness, "one of the reasons I came to Ballinamore was to see whether we could take up where we left off. I've never met anyone like you since. An hour in your company is worth ten in anyone else's. Now, don't look so worried. I don't mean to plunge into anything all of a sudden. We could take it easy, see each other once a week to begin with. Whatever suits you. Think about it anyway."

I really didn't need to. Anyone who was obsessed with dead people, with the past, had a problem with the present and the living. I wasn't qualified to dig deeply into Eddie's psyche and see why that was so. And yet, it was tempting to have company that could talk back, someone who appreciated me.

"I'll think about it, Eddie," I said. "And thank you for those nice things you said about me. It's lovely to hear them."

Nanny was unexpectedly heavy. I didn't like the way her head hung and swung about when we lifted her, so I fetched a blanket and put her on it. It took us all our time to carry her to where Eddie had dug a hole underneath the Cox's Pippin. We lowered her into it.

"Do you want to, em, say anything?" Eddie asked quietly. He was a sensitive creature really.

A band like steel clutched my throat.

"Thank you, Nanny. For being you. For loving me." For your floppy ears, your wet nose against my face as we sat in the sun, the little whickers for apples.

I could feel Eddie give me a look but I didn't dare return it. Bones were what he preferred. They don't answer back.

After a cup of hot chocolate and a caramel slice, Eddie

decided to go. It was a sad parting. I felt I had let go of something I valued in the past, a me I was no longer in touch with. Eddie fumbled his good-bye, as usual.

"You're sure you'll be all right? I'd like to stay, to . . . you know . . . talk about old times," he said. I opened the car door and he climbed in. As he closed the door, he paused. "Never be the same again, would it?"

I hadn't the heart to agree with him.

"Put that somewhere cold," Noreen said, handing me a bottle of wine wrapped in Christmas paper and tied with tinsel.

"And put that one somewhere hot," Seamus said in his usual meaningful way, thrusting a bottle of whiskey at my chest. He was always the first to arrive so that he could take up his usual position beside the cocktail cabinet.

"And put this," he said, taking a sprig of mistletoe from his pocket, "somewhere handy."

I could think of one or two places I'd like to have put it but it was Christmas, so I restrained myself and hid it behind the piano.

Noreen poured us both a G & T. Seamus helped himself to a tumbler of whiskey.

"Well, if you'll both excuse me, I'll just take a look to see what's burning."

Once in the kitchen, I took a few lungsful of air and felt a little better. I wondered why on earth I was putting myself through all this instead of having a quiet evening by the fire. The rice was cooked and the stew smelt delicious. I took a peek through a hole in the door where a knot of wood was missing. The room was filling up. PJ from next door was there with his wife. A stout little thing who never seemed to leave the kitchen except to throw some scraps to the hens. I felt the way I used to before an examination: butterflies in the tummy, headache and bowel trouble. I mused on old J P Sartre's aphorism, "Hell is other people" and braved my way into the fray.

No sooner were we into discussing the festering season than the door opened. Gaye and Percy Greene and Dunkie. Gaye, resplendent in a pink maternity top with white spots, came forward and kissed me on the cheek.

"Not really big enough yet," she said, patting her tummy, "but I couldn't resist it," she whispered as I led her into the room.

"Now gentlemen, help yourselves," I said pointing to the cocktail cabinet against which Seamus hung like a Minotaur guarding the labyrinth.

Gaye winked and took my arm. "Let me give you a hand in the kitchen."

"Great news, Philippa," Gaye went on. "I had a scan and the baby is okay. Just thirteen weeks old. They let me see it, its little heart beating away and waggling its arms and legs. So tiny. I got a photograph of it and Percy got it-framed. Don't forget, as far as everyone else is concerned, Dunkie is just a friend."

I nodded, half afraid to speak. Life was becoming too complicated already. The phone rang.

"Would you rescue the mince pies, Gaye."

"Sorry, Philippa. Not allowed to lift anything heavier than a bird's nest," she said, taking off for the sitting-room.

"Hello."

Emily.

"Don't worry, Philly, we're coming. I was just phoning to ask if you would mind if we brought along our new neighbours. Seem like an interesting pair. She's interested in art. He's in business."

"Of course. Plenty of food. So hurry along."

Perhaps I ought to have put out the Picasso print I picked up in Antibes and the Susie Cooper plate. But then Emily sometimes gets the wrong end of the stick. The woman may only be a watercolourist, dabbling at still life while the children are at school. How I hanker for really civilised company.

I collected the platters from the kitchen table and undid the clingfilm. Smoked salmon, thin slices of steamed pork with slices of mushroom, Philippa's Pâté, of course, pears with cheese and a pile of other delicacies I'd spent days preparing.

The room had filled in my absence.

"My goodness, you've gone to a lot of trouble." Clara. I was taken aback by her compliment. She even smiled.

"Oh it's nothing. I just threw a few things together this afternoon."

"I hope there won't be any bad feeling, Philippa. Eddie and I are going on holiday together."

"He's invited you away with him?"

"A bit of a coincidence, though I'm sure it wouldn't have been long before we got together anyway. I phoned to thank him for coming to the meeting and I just happened to mention how I hated Christmas and planned to go to Morocco."

Cheaper than the Canaries. Eddie must be mad.

"Well, I hope you both have a wonderful time. Although Eddie's idea of a perfect holiday is digging up bones. Be sure to stay upright at all times. Sausage roll?"

Clara has no sense of humour.

"Sorry we're so late," Emily said breathlessly and with a string of people in tow. The glamorous one must be the new neighbour.

"Let me introduce you to Sophia Delacy."

A long, slim sparkling hand shot towards me. In the nick of time, I handed Emily the plate of sausage rolls. Sophia flashed a set of crowns and tossed back her shoulder-length hair, flicked out, a style I thought went out with the ark.

"All one word – Delacy. Delighted to meet you. Emily has told us so much about you."

Emily really thinks I'm some sort of freakshow. I'll have to try to be as boring as possible.

Robert Delacy was introduced next, a Balkan Sobranie Black Russian in his mouth, the smoke curling up between a pair of black eyes.

"How are you?" he asked. One of those people who puts the onus on anyone but themselves.

"Wonderful," I smiled as sincerely as I could, "and you?"

"Fine. Fine. Mustn't grumble. A lot to be thankful for. Think positive. None of this negative crap," he added, sucking on the cigarette for all he was worth.

Indeed. I wondered what on earth he was hiding. Emily will no doubt hear it all in due course. Sophia looked the confessional type.

Most of the tidbits had disappeared, along with a considerable quantity of gin and whiskey that Seamus was dispensing along with his seasonal bonhomie. So long as he was busy he couldn't get up to anything. Next was the main course. Stewed kid in port with peas. Of course, I pretended it was lamb so as not to upset anyone's sensibilities, though they're probably the sort of people who buy puppies at Christmas and kick the animal out when it starts to grow up.

Dunkie was in the kitchen fondling the twins.

"Orphans? I thought so. They sucked my finger. I'll feed them for you, if you like."

"That would be a help," I said, "the one with the white stripe down its nose is a bit tricky."

"Don't worry. I spent half my time at this lark when I was a boy. My parents had a dairy farm, a herd of thirty Friesian cows. They went down time after time with TB."

"That must have been difficult," I said by way of encouragement.

"Father got a bit fed up with the whole thing, sold them and bought in-calf heifers to start a suckler herd. Unfortunately, they'd been put to too big a bull, the calves were huge. You can guess the rest. We lost all but two."

"What a shame! How heartbreaking . . ."

"First time I ever saw my parents cry. They sold up and came to live in the city. But never settled. Miserable till they died. Couldn't adjust to having people all round them, noise, car fumes, supermarket food."

He lifted one of the kids from its bed and began to hug it.

"Nothing like the space of a few fields, the smell of animals."

"Yes. I know what you mean. With me, it was the other way round. I began with the noise, fumes and concrete jungle and escaped to here."

"You look very happy when you say that. Your face lights up."

I could see why Gaye Greene fell for this fellow. Definitely simpatico.

"As soon as you've finished, come in before the locusts have descended on the casserole. It's really kid but I'm pretending it's lamb," I whispered. "Don't say a word or I'll sick the pigs onto you," I warned.

All the girls, except Gaye, came to help, just like we do on our picnics. Clara was the rice person and Emily and Noreen dished out the stew. The others passed the plates around. Sophia was in the background, waxing lyrical about something or other, her voice carrying like a loudspeaker at a fairground.

"I just love *mange tout*. So fresh, so crisp in texture."

"I think they're completely overrated. Like chewing bits of pea pod," I said to no one in particular.

"You can't be growing them properly, Philippa. Plenty of

126

kitchen waste in November and a good dose of FYM before planting."

I decided not to be rude to a guest.

"There's plenty of wine everyone, red and white. I think, Seamus, you can retire from bar duty for the moment."

He shot me a bleary-eyed look.

"Yes, Ma'am," he saluted.

Sozzled already. So long as he was taken quietly away when he collapsed.

We all sat down and tucked in. It was remarkably good.

"Do you know where I ate the best lamb stew in my life? Don't you remember, Dahling?" Sophia again. "Greece. On my Classical Tour. We had just come from the caryatids, probably the last people to be allowed within a stone's throw of them, with our guide, Andreas, who never let me out of his sight. Rather embarrassing really. Took us to a tiny little inn where we were greeted by the most charming couple you could meet, so sincere and simple, peasants of course, and they brought us into the most beautiful little room, wooden beams, fresh flowers everywhere, lace tablecloths and napkins and served this wonderful stew. We tucked into it as if we'd just come off a desert island."

"Well, don't let this one get cold!" I said as pleasantly as I could.

I felt the room heave a sight of relief. Glasses were refilled. Gaye Greene and Dunkie were giggling in a corner. I made the only comment I felt worthwhile, just to keep the conversation going:

"Of course, they don't eat lamb in Greece. Goat is the national dish."

"Of course, of course," Robert "Dahling" said. "Got to get the facts right, Sophia dear. Can't argue with those."

"What does it matter?" Sophia shrugged. "It's like one of

127

my clients asking whether a painting is a "real" Paul Henry or whether a plate is hand-painted or merely laid with transfers. What does it matter if you like it?"

"I suppose a fella wouldn't be expected to pay the same sort of money if it wasn't the genuine article." Seamus's grasp of the core of the matter surprised me. The stew must have had a sobering effect.

"Besides," I decided to interject a serious note, "there is a joy in holding and looking at a work of art one knows has been painted by a particular artist that cannot be had from a mere imitation."

Clara and Noreen smiled. Emily shifted a bit and said, "Sophia has a huge collection of all sorts of pictures; she's even written a book about it all."

Sophia made a mock-modest squirm as if to shrug it off.

"Oh, that was a year or two ago," she said. "*Climate and the Painter*. I tried to show the influence of climate, rain, snow, wind, fog. I came up with some startling conclusions."

Seamus came around to top up the wine, a bottle in each hand.

"Well now, Soph-eye-a," he said, "I often made the same conclusions myself. Many's the time I said to Noreen, the wife here, how it's the devil's own job to get paint to dry on a foggy Saturday. But she stands at the bottom of the ladder and threatens to wiggle it if I don't get a move on! What do ye think of that now. A woman that would wiggle your ladder would be capable of anything."

I decided it was time for dessert; strawberry sorbet with boudoir biscuits for those whose teeth could stand the cold. For those who were more sensitive, there were chocolate profiteroles. Percy and Dunkie attended to Gaye like drones flapping about a queen bee, bringing her tidbits, coaxing a tasty morsel here, a sip of raspberry cordial there. Noreen had some words with Seamus who managed to stand up and lurched towards the desserts. Teresa and

Dotty, having slipped in quietly as usual, were already in front of them.

"We thought we'd try a bit of everything," Dotty twittered.

Nothing like a bit of adventure at Christmas-time.

By ten o'clock I was thoroughly fed up with everyone and went to chat to the kids. No Nanny to tell my woes to any more. No little whickers of understanding. Only Sophia's husband, staring down at the sleeping kids in the oven drawer.

"Rather fetching at that age," he said. I smiled at him as best I could. "Pity they grow up to be such ugly brutes. Still, mustn't grumble. Everything has its purpose."

He seemed to doubt it or to want reassurance.

"Nature abhors a vacuum," I added helpfully.

"Just what I was thinking. A woman after my own heart."

Here we go. Next it would be "my wife doesn't understand me".

"Sophia wouldn't agree but it's all part of one great design. Take business. One business fails, another steps in to take its place. There's room for everything. It's competition at its most positive. Not so much the survival of the fittest but the survival of what nature deems necessary to continue."

Quite. "Well, if you'll excuse me there's a rum baba getting cold and a trifle melting. Do come in when you're ready."

I hurried towards the sweet trolley. Sophia was holding forth. Still. The others were sunk into their cushions, ladling the dessert into them. I could see why Dahling had to keep so positive. One little slip into negativity and he'd throttle her. Seamus looked at a dangerously intoxicated stage, his face bright red and an inch of ash drooping at the end of his cigarette. Teresa and Dotty were finished first and were now busy examining the material on the couch. I could have told them it was nothing but the best printed Provençal cotton straight from the looms at Soleido. Dickie and Emily were staring into space and sipping their wine. Gaye, Percy and Dunkie were obviously enjoying themselves in a corner, whispering to each other. PJ and his wife were still on the couch, silent as stone. Sophia droned on and on.

"Will I get it, Philippa?" Emily asked.

You can live in hope, I felt like replying.

"The doorbell," she added.

"Please do. I didn't hear it."

An enormous bunch of flowers came into the room closely followed by someone tall and dark against the light. The rum baba fell from my hands. PJ's wife rushed over to me to pick it up, closely followed by the figure in black. It was Gerald.

"Only got your invitation yesterday. Just had time to clear everything and catch the plane."

"Care for some baby rum – I mean rum baba. Just the thing after a long journey. Excuse me till I get a cloth."

"Let me take your coat," I heard Clara say as I wobbled to the kitchen. What a turn-up for the books! People should really know when they're not supposed to take an invitation seriously, when it's meant merely as a gesture to let them know you'd like them to come but of course you would never expect to see them. What's he going to think of that mob? "Show me your friends and I'll show you the real you," the nuns always said. But then Gerald is probably a Protestant. He wouldn't know about any of that.

With difficulty, I tried to breathe and put on my façade as I returned with the cloth. PJ's wife grabbed it and began scrubbing at the carpet.

"What sort of books do you write?" Clara asked, acting the queen bee, *ça va sans dire*. I rushed to Gerald's aid.

"Now, now we mustn't trouble a weary traveller with forty questions, Clara. Come to the fire and warm yourself. Emily – be a dear and reheat some stew. I'll have a mulled wine for you in a jiffy."

The mulled wine was to be a nightcap but now was as good a time as any. I pulled out the little cast-iron plate arrangement attached to the old crane I got PJ to fix up for me on one of his visits. I put the pot on top of this with red wine, honey, spices and a tot of brandy.

"The aroma is enough to intoxicate," Gerald looked at me, smiling. He seemed pleased to see me. I felt cheered up no end.

Not to be outdone, Clara brought the food. Soon everyone gathered about the fire, pulling down cushions to the floor. Someone turned off the lights. It's amazing how handsome even the plainest look in firelight. Perhaps a throwback to when nature had to force us to breed, no matter what. At night all cats are grey.

Dunkie began to poke the embers and piled on some more wood.

"Reminds me of home. It used to be my job to keep the fire going. You'd to damp it down at night, just enough so it would light up again in the morning. Woe betide you if it didn't! There were no firelighters in our house. You'd to go into the barn and bring in some straw and twist a few strands of it and coax whatever red you could find to burn. But the dinners that came off it! Never tasted better – except for your goat stew, Philly." Silly man let the cat out of the bag. "Not poor old Nanny, I hope?" Gerald looked at me in consternation. The others were taken aback.

"Lamb, I thought you said. Wasn't it lamb, Dahling?" Sophia, eyes wide and her hand over her mouth for once.

"Sure it's all the wan," Seamus said from the depths of somewhere. "Meat. Lucky it isn't head soup like some folk are so fond of in America. Sure, God knows what's in them hamburgers. Bulls ba–"

"That's enough, Seamus!" Noreen swiped his glass from him. "They say it's one hundred per cent beef."

"That just means it isn't plastic, or glass, or wood." He leaned forward slightly. "It could be ears or noses or bal–"

"Seamus!" Noreen shouted again.

Dahling shifted uneasily. "All part of the planet anyway. Nothing abhorrent in nature. It's all what you believe," he said sagely, trying desperately to reassure himself.

"Begob, a body would die of turst around here."

"Here you are, you poor dear," Sophia said, jumping up to give Seamus a glass of mulled wine. On top of all the G & T it would be an interesting mixture.

"That's a grand girl ye have there," Seamus nudged Dahling who said nothing but drank his mulled wine rather quickly. At this rate I would be running out.

"Cheers," Gerald said, raising his glass. He looked almost good-looking in the firelight with his yellow silk shirt, open at the neck, and brown suede waistcoat. His hand lay on my shoulder. I wished I didn't enjoy it being there so much. The human is full of yearnings and hopes and longings. Are they ever fulfilled? I looked at Gaye Greene. There was something nice happening for her, anyway. With a heavy heart I finished dishing out the dessert. Sweetmeats as a substitute for a warm glow inside, to fill the void. I sat back into a dark corner by the fire near Gerald. The others were busy eating and getting giddy on the mulled wine.

"You've gone very quiet," Gerald whispered.

"Just thinking," I said. "Sometimes when I see other people with such sadness written all over their face, so unhappy, I wonder what it's all about."

"That's your own sadness you see, Philippa."

"No, it's only when I look at them I feel it."

"It may be sparked off by looking but it's inside you too."

"It makes me not want to be near anyone, to run a mile."

"You feel like running from yourself, your sadness?"

"Of course. Don't we all? What's the point in dwelling on it? It just makes it worse."

"Sometimes if we stay with it and face it, it diminishes. Same with writing. Sometimes things don't come right and I'd say, oh, it's not working. Change it. But then often something would prompt me to take another look and strangely, when I did, I would find my view expanded, my vision greater."

"You must be very brave, Gerald. I'm not sure I have that sort of courage."

"But you're aware of what it takes."

"So I can't be all bad. Is that it?"

"I think you're terrific."

How come when someone nice says something really generous we wonder what they're up to? With Gerald it wasn't sex because he could have had me "on toast" in Bath; it wasn't money because he obviously had plenty. Could it be the Gods had forgiven me for Jack's death and were smiling on me at last?

The room had gone suddenly quiet. The crock with the mulled wine was empty. Bodies everywhere with glazed expressions on their faces. Hot, tired and quietly sozzled. So much for jolly Christmas parties.

"I haven't booked a bed anywhere," Gerald said, *à propos* nothing. "Don't suppose you know of a quiet little boarding house hereabouts?" The man was reading my mind again. Must remember not to think about crisp sheets and naked bodies.

"I've plenty of room here, if you'd care to share a house with a spinster graduate of the Holborne and two little kiddies."

"I would be delighted."

133

The pink room, definitely. It was filled with the perfume of lavender and burnet rose buds I picked and dried last spring.

It was long past bedtime. Everyone looked sleepy but with no sign of leaving. Perhaps if I brought out some expensive goodies from *Philippa's Pantry* or closed the cocktail cabinet they would take the hint.

"I just hate to see a good party go to waste," said Sophia, already twigging. "Why don't we all gather ourselves and repair to Hawthorn? Plenty of champers in the fridge and I dare say we could find a snack or two, eh Dahling? A bit of cold lamb, perhaps? Turn it into a bit of a house-warming." Not even the sparkle of her designer teeth could elicit a shred of enthusiasm.

Everyone looked at the carpet. However, it would be rude to refuse to play at house-warming really, especially if Sophia was going to be part and parcel of the landscape in the years to come. Not to mention the promise of champagne.

"Yes, do come," Dahling said after a nudge in the ribs from Sophia. "It will make the house looked lived-in."

Plenty of ash from Seamus and spilt champagne – just the thing.

"And you too, of course, Miss Woodcock, are most welcome," Sophia said, sincere only in her insincerity.

"I'll take a raincheck on that," I said yawning.

"You'll be very interested to see our collection of first editions, Gerald," Piranha Teeth said, gathering her stiff limbs together.

"Not tonight, Sophia," Gerald said firmly, "thank you just the same. Perhaps another time." No excuses. Always the gentleman.

Like snow off a ditch, they were gone. Even Seamus managed to shuffle to the door, already tasting the bubbles.

Plates of pastry crust, half-eaten trifle and unidentifiable heaps were left beside empty, well-fingered glasses. So much for gratitude and loyalty. Eat it, drink it and scarper. Who cares?

Gerald was beside the fire, raking it through and piling it with turf and sticks.

"I'll put the kettle on for a nightcap," I smiled.

"I'll give you a hand," he said, standing up and following me to the kitchen.

"I love your little 'nest'. Cosy and warm yet sophisticated."

"I had a head start, really, because it was always an actual house. So many people have bought barns and stables and expect to make them look like somewhere to live. To me they still look as if the hay and the horse have just left and someone has slapped a bit of paint on the walls to take the harm out of it."

"Nothing escapes you, Philippa. You have an eye for the absurd."

"The 'sewers on the beach', my family used to say."

"Sounds more like reality to me. No one seems to want much of it. An unpopular role you've taken on."

"You make it sound as if it's deliberate. It's just the way I see things."

I put a generous tot of whiskey into my best crystal, a wedge of lemon embedded with cloves and a dollop of honey.

"Just what my mother always ordered for a chilly night, lemon and honey," Gerald said, giving me a wink as he took a sip.

"Delicious. By the by, thank you for inviting me. You did want me to come?"

"Of course I did. I wouldn't dream of wasting money on a stamp for nothing."

I'd like to have said "I'm glad you did" but sipped in silence instead.

"I'll bring you to your room as soon as I've locked up.

It's the pink one. It gets the morning sun."

Silence.

"Thank you," he said, not looking at me.

I put the kettle on again for hot-water bottles, fed the kids, and went outside to shut the ducks in for the night. The air was crisp, the sky clear with a sliver of moon in its last quarter.

"You can see the Milky Way," Gerald said in the dark behind me. I nearly jumped out of my skin.

"Sorry. I'm used to four-legged company. Two legs startle me."

"My apologies. I tried to be as quiet as I could."

He held my shoulders, put his arms around my back and pulled me gently towards him.

Minutes later, we stood watching the sky and saw the shooting star.

"Make a wish, make a wish," I urged him.

"I made one a few months ago when I was on holiday in Aran. It's still the same."

I didn't dare enquire any further. Life is full of disappointments. I prefer to travel in hope.

I put the lights out and led the way upstairs.

"The window in your room is still open, Gerald, you might wish to shut it. I prefer a breath of air if I'm snug under the duvet."

"I'm a hothouse plant, I'm afraid. Product of a fussy mother, thermal vests and long johns until May. She thought central heating the ultimate in unhealthiness, so it was coal fires everywhere. I'm allergic to sulphur ever since. Can't even abide eggs."

What a funny character. *Cherchez la mère* and you'll find the son. I always advise people contemplating matrimony to look deeply into the family. It usually means the whole thing is postponed while everyone goes for therapy.

I put on the light in the pink room and drew the

curtains. Gerald cast an appreciative glance around. He had no luggage with him. One of those who slept in the nude and ruined the sheets. I always use linen ones. They're as cold "as if an elephant had pissed on them" Jack used to say but they wash beautifully and dry in next to no time. Necessary qualities if an elephant did happen to despoil them.

I put the hot-water bottle in the bed and turned down the covers. Gerald already had his jacket off and hanging in the wardrobe. He was busy undoing his cuff links and looking very intently at me.

"There's plenty of hot water for a bath, if you wish," I said to fill the gap. "Towels in the hot press."

"I'm sure I'll be most comfortable. It's your house, after all."

There was a noise in the distance. The phone.

"I think someone's trying to reach you," Gerald smiled.

"That's what I'm afraid of," I said as I opened the door; "you would think at this time of the night everyone would be safely tucked into bed."

Except for Agatha, that is.

"Pippy? Thought I'd never get you. You'll never guess what's happened!"

The sky has fallen down, she's won the Lotto, she hasn't had a drink for half an hour.

"It's Andrew," she said breathlessly. "He's back home. After all these years."

She was raving again.

"You wouldn't know him. All craggy-faced, with the most dreadful Australian accent. He says the Abos are the nicest people you could meet, even if they eat slugs and snails. He says they're delicious. Anyway, he's staying for Christmas," she went on without a pause for breath. "I said you'd be delighted to see him. We'll probably be down on Christmas Eve. Don't go to any trouble. I'll make the gravy."

137

Gravy is my pet aversion. It reminds me of the stuff used to point bricks. Agatha can't live without it, heavily laced with sherry.

I hung up and very slowly dragged myself to bed. I glanced towards the pink room. The gap at the door saddle was black as night. Fortunately, I don't own a dog. It would have got very rough treatment.

The morning was cold; the grass white with frost. The animals would be hungry. Perhaps Gerald would carry some hay for me.

I put on a big, slap-up breakfast: rashers, sausages, home-made black pudding and eggs. All this talk of cholesterol and frying is absolute rubbish. If only people realised that cooking with vegetable or nut oils is actually good for them, supplying a different form of fat, they wouldn't know themselves. It's sugar that's the killer, forming cholesterol is its business. But if I said that out loud, the beet farmers would be up in arms.

"What a wonderful smell, Philippa. It woke me up."

"Proust said it was our strongest sense. There is a smell of dried earth and parsley that reminds me of shopping for vegetables with my mother."

"It must be nice to have good memories of one's childhood."

"If they were good. I won't bore you with the horrors of it."

"Philippa," he said gently, coming towards me, "I would never be bored by you."

What a nice man. It would be lovely to really believe him.

From the barn we took a bale of hay and half a sack of rolled barley. It was a day for the tractor. I hated the thing, big, noisy and dangerous. But useful. Gerald put the food in the transport box.

"Would you like me to drive?" he asked.

"Thought you'd never offer! Seriously, I didn't know you could drive one of these."

"Had to, in Africa as part of my stint helping a village to grow crops and dig irrigation channels. Two of the best years of my life. I love black people."

"Yes, they're so beautiful, so creative, so magnificent. I've never been to Africa."

"Yes, I'd like to go back again. Perhaps we'll get there."

Like an expert, Gerald steered the tractor through the yard and down towards the wood.

Poppy heard the tractor and made a beeline for us, her calf trotting at her heels. The sheep were huddled under a spreading ash tree, baaing like mad. They could probably smell the barley.

We stopped, put the hay in the rack and the barley in the feeding troughs.

"Hang on," I said, "there's a sheep missing."

"How on earth can you count them when they won't stay still?"

"You count their legs and divide by four."

"Very *drôle*."

Except that there was nothing funny about a missing sheep. One always imagined the worst, lying in a ditch with its legs in the air, eyes pecked out by crows.

"Where on earth are you off to?" Gerald asked as I sprinted towards the wood.

"To look for the one that's missing."

"You could at least say that and allow me to help. But that's not your style, is it, Philippa? You prefer to go it alone."

"This is not the time to discuss my *modus vivendi*. The sheep may be dead."

"If so, there is no point in us tearing off after it."

He was angry now. I pressed on like someone demented.

He just didn't understand. I had to know.

It was impossible to see in the wood, the trees like looming black presences. Nothing for it but to go through it, tree by tree.

At the edge of the wood, where the bluebells carpet the ground in spring, something moved. I stopped for Gerald to catch up with me.

"Think I see her, down there beneath the crab apple."

"I'm afraid, without its leaves, I can't tell one tree from another. Like trying to tell naked women apart when their faces are covered."

I ignored the comparison and walked forward. Of course, the silly animal moved again but circled back.

"Ah. Must have a lamb. She's not keen to leave the place."

We walked slowly towards her and there on the ground was a collection of legs and heads in a snug bundle.

"Triplets, Philippa."

I looked at him to see whether I had heard correctly.

"I counted their legs!" he said, pleased as punch he'd got his own back.

"We'd better leave them alone for a few hours to get used to the big, bad world. Come back when they've got to their feet and have been fed. I'll probably have to take one of them away and feed it."

Terrific. Two kids and a lamb to keep me busy for the next six months.

"Nature in the raw," he said as he planted a kiss on my cheek. I turned and looked and kissed him back. On the lips. I pressed my back into a tree for support and regretted the frosty ground.

"Shame I've to go back today, Philippa. But I'd like to pay another visit, if I may."

I was so cross I almost said not to bother, but I turned towards the tractor instead. Whatever was happening in his life was more important than me.

Yet he had come.

"I really would like to come back," he squeezed my hands.

"Of course you may. In spring, when the bluebells are in bloom."

In the meantime, I had Christmas with Aggie and Andrew to look forward to. Even the Canaries was beginning to look attractive. If only. If only Gerald would whisk me back to London, or Bath or even anywhere.

"I hate Christmas," Agatha said as soon as she arrived. "I wish they would cancel it. All the fuss and expense. Still, at least this year, we'll all be together," she said, her arm outstretched towards her Citroen where a tall, lanky figure, reminiscent of my father, was trying to extricate himself.

"He's changed a bit," Agatha whispered, "but he's still our brother." Families have a habit of forcing you into accepting the unacceptable.

"G'day, sport." He tossed his kit-bag on the doorstep and pumped my arm.

I settled for "How are you?" and ushered him into the hallway.

"All the better for seeing you!" he replied.

Terrific.

Feeling completely at home, he ambled towards my favourite perch by the fire and sat down heavily, flinging his boots into the fireplace.

"What do you think of Pippy's little abode, Andy?" Agatha enquired.

"Fair dinkum."

If this went on, I would need a translator. Perhaps it was better not to know. I felt like killing Agatha for sicking this ghost from the miserable past onto me.

She followed me to the kitchen.

"I'm just great now, Pippy. All those electric shocks worked a treat. They must have released something."

They say people are so thrilled they survive them, they think they're cured. Give it six weeks.

"Speaking about release, how long is your friend staying?" I said, putting on the kettle.

"He's our brother, Pippy. Nothing can change that. We owe him that recognition."

"That and no more. I don't feel the least bit of attachment to him. He hasn't changed one iota, still the same charming bastard who called me 'fish eyes' as a child." I turned off the tap a little more tightly than was necessary. "I'd still like to know how long I've to put with him."

"Pippy, your language is dreadful. Must be living in the country, playing with animals that does it." As usual, she avoided answering a straight question.

I slammed the kettle on the hob and decided against offering any of my caramel slices.

"I'm going to be very busy, Agatha. I've a lot of cooking to do and I hate anyone watching, so if you don't mind."

Seeing you like the creep so much, you entertain him.

"You're so rejecting, Pippy. I feel you don't want me," she said as she walked out of the kitchen and closed the door behind her.

Through the missing knot in the door, I watched her open the cupboard and empty most of a bottle of whiskey into two glasses. She handed one to Andy, mouthing some obscenities and scowling towards the kitchen.

Whoever did the ECT job put the electrodes in the wrong place. Perhaps the machine needed to be re-calibrated.

Christmas Eve arrived, mild and windy. I went out early in the morning and stayed out longer than the chores demanded. Nanny's kids were now sharing quarters with the triplet lamb, head-butting each other at every opportunity. Aggression's in the marrow of all animals. A set of twins, born the previous evening, were finding their way to the milk bar, sucking tail, hair, anything that looked promising. If they didn't find the right part quickly, it would be too late to establish their sucking reflex or for their mother's colostrum to work.

Feeling anxious, I left them to it and wandered towards the wood. Though leafless, the branches of the trees were still full of colour, grey-brown, carrying the red twigs of last year's growth. Holly, the "magic" tree, stood green and shining, the berries all eaten by hungry birds, its wood no longer in demand for cart shafts. Robin Redbreast was busy nibbling the remains of the haws, a great delicacy with the Chinese, who coat them in toffee. Strange that so much that is found in the fields has become defiled, like snails and dandelion leaves. Even the poor old blackberry is left to rot on the cane. Everyone is too busy watching television.

"What, Pip, no TV? You gone crook or something?" Andrew greeted me on my return. "What in hell do you do with yourself?"

"I lead a perfectly normal, worthwhile and fulfilled life without one."

"Don't that beat everything, Aggie?"

"Perhaps, Andy, if Pips knew you were coming she'd have organised one," said Agatha, her speech distinctly garbled.

"I most certainly would not. I presume it was to chat to me you came, not to watch the box."

"Listen, mate, don't come the raw prawn with me. I just asked."

And it was only Christmas Eve.

Christmas morning was wet, windy and cold. I put the ducks in the oven for a long, slow cook. All the well-known chefs say to give them about an hour and a half.

Not being partial to raw duck, I cook them until the skin is dark and crisp.

"Not your little quackers, Philippa," Agatha whined as I pricked the skins to let the fat escape.

"You know it upsets me."

"If you wish, stick to the stuffing and vegetables. I would hazard a guess that our fraternal relation could polish off several ducks at one sitting. He'd be delighted to eat your portion."

"I suppose I better eat something. I don't really enjoy my food. There are times when I just can't eat, so it's Complan."

I made a face.

"If you take it through a straw it's not too bad. Mummy used to call it 'liquid cement'. Poor Mummy. I miss them at Christmas."

"I'm afraid I don't miss all the carry-on and drinking and sulking. I prefer to enjoy Christmas on my own."

"I knew you didn't really want me. I should have stayed at home. The Gilligans next door invited me for Christmas lunch but all that shopping for presents really put me off. I just couldn't be bothered. And the expense of it. I thought you'd like to see your brother, after all he hasn't been home for fifteen years."

"Such a short time in a different country. It takes a lifetime to get settled in. He's only teasing himself by coming home now."

And annoying the rest of us.

"He's considering not going back. Says he'd like to settle in a rural area. You don't happen to know of any farms for sale around here? Something that's maybe a bit run-down and going cheap. Andy would enjoy clearing the land. That's what he did in the bush."

"There isn't a thing that doesn't cost the earth and the Midlands is not the bush."

145

"I shouldn't have bothered asking you. 'I'm all right Jack' is your motto. It was the same when you got Daddy's stamp album. He meant *me* to have it; I was always his 'little girl'."

"Only because he was too drunk to remember your name."

That did it. She left the kitchen in high dudgeon. All I needed was for both of them to lay claim to my little holding, like magpies taking the eyes from a still breathing lamb. I owed them nothing.

Lunch was memorable only for the row of "beer tubes" the brother lined up on the table. At dessert he tried to knock them down by blowing grape pips at them. Agatha found this highly amusing, helped by copious quantities of wine. I took out the book I had bought myself for Christmas, *The Tibetan Book of Living and Dying*, to try to find some solace. It urged more compassion than I felt but then we can't always be perfect.

At three the phone rang.

"A Merry Christmas, Philippa. I hope you're enjoying yourself."

Gerald.

"And many happy returns. Your festivities couldn't be worse than mine. I'm afraid the remnants of the Woodcocks are here. All two of them. An absolute crowd."

"Oh, I do see."

"You understand?"

"Of course. Nothing more likely to depress the living daylights out of you than a dose of relations. They think they can drop the normal rudiments of civilised behaviour, while expecting you to treat them like a prized guest!"

"You seem to be speaking from the heart, Gerald."

"I'm afraid so. I'm at the ancestral with father and big sister, who has come to bully the old man into eating his veg and making sure I fly right. The wimp, as she laughingly calls her husband, spends his time with his Yorkshire terrier. Their anaemic offspring spends all her time in bed. Father's his usual charming self, tipping cigarette ash into his trouser turn-ups, knocking back the gin. I seem to be going on a bit. They must be getting to me."

"I'm glad you've a shoulder to cry on even if it is only me."

"Don't put yourself down like that, Philippa. I'll get very cross."

"I feel such a heel. I feel I should like Aggie and Andy because they're my family. But they're so obnoxious, I'm finding it impossible. How come they both seem to have reasonably civilised friends and a good social life?"

"Ah, because we save our worst side for our family."

After some minutes silence for the death of familial love, he said, "I'm really looking forward to seeing the bluebells in the wood. The offer is still open, I presume?"

"Of course." I had temporarily forgotten. Perhaps we would manage a few days on our own.

Gerald's words echoed and re-echoed during the following week. Andy grew more and more bored and therefore more critical.

"Why the hell don't you put those animals into a barn? Save all that trekking up and down and watching and minding."

I didn't bother explaining that I felt they were happier being outside, as well as healthier. Besides, I enjoyed the trekking. It got me out of the house, especially when there were undesirables in it. I was even grateful to the pigs for needing food four times a day.

When the gin ran out, Aggie took to the mead, which she felt needed a bit of bite to it. So she mixed it with whiskey. Her mornings began at two pm with a glass of Complan and a fist of paracetamol.

"Need some wood chopped?" Andrew asked one morning. Boredom was really getting to him.

"Thought you'd never ask."

I took him to the wood where the rest of the ash tree lay on the ground, too big for my little saw. He set to it with an axe. Each stroke followed the last in a steady rhythm. He grew warm in the still air and removed his shirt. His body was well muscled and bronzed, except for a white scar across his back. A memory was jogged of a knocked over glass of whiskey and the screams of a ten-year-old Andy that would have stripped wallpaper. And I thought about Agatha and her unhappiness. And then I thought about me. Our scars connected us, making the past present.

"Sure you're not overdoing it?" I asked him. He looked at me as if I had two heads.

"Ye know, Sis, you don't look half bad when your face is all soft."

I supposed that was a compliment.

"Maybe," he said, picking up a piece of wood and examining it intently, "maybe, I haven't been an exactly model guest. Coming back . . . and all that . . . Hasn't been exactly hunky-dory."

"I think I know what you mean."

Andy chopped the last of the wood and I stacked it in the wheelbarrow. He pulled it towards the house while I pushed from behind.

"I'll bring some in and build up the fire," he said, putting on his shirt, "Ag's probably let it go out."

"After that we'll have a nice hot whiskey and a piece of Christmas cake."

Agatha was curled up on the couch, looking a ghostly shade of green, her skin taut and wrinkled from dehydration.

"She looks really ill, Andy." I tried to keep the alarm out of my voice.

"Too much of the sauce. Boy, does she mix 'em," he said, in apparent admiration.

"I'm afraid our Agatha has a serious drink problem. She thinks it's depression or the state of the planet, or anything else except drink. She just won't listen."

"I met an Aussie alco once. He said it wasn't till he'd hit rock bottom he decided he'd had enough. Poor old Aggie ain't that far gone yet, I guess."

"I'm afraid her liver will be gone before the truth dawns. Her brain must be the size of a pea."

"How long has this been going on?"

"Since Mummy died. Agatha never got over it. She said she hated Mother so much, she killed her. Metaphorically speaking. As you know, Mother was actually run over by the 49A bus on her way to collect her pension. At the funeral the priest assured me she was 'in a state of grace' when she was mown down and would certainly pass straight through the pearly gates. How he knew beats me. Perhaps he was just trying to reassure me."

"Whatever about pearly gates, it'll be a pine box for little old Aggie if we don't get her to a hospital."

"You think she's that bad?"

"The symptoms all fit. Too much liquor. Body working overtime to clear it out. We'll have to try waking her up, get some liquid into her."

I got a jug of water and a glass. Andy propped her up and began to slap at her cheeks. Like trying to wake the dead. The more I looked at her, the more I realised something drastic would have to be done. I called the doctor and arranged a bed for her. Not St Jude's. They would simply pamper her. It would have to be St Brendan's. Perhaps the shock would perform some miracle.

"I'm so glad you're here, Andy. It is a relief," I said, surprising even myself.

He looked at me and sighed. "Thanks," he said, nodding

and then that warm, expansive smile.

"You've been through a hard time with little sister, eh? We'll both give her a good talking-to when she snaps out of this."

"It sounds too good to be true. For the first time in my life I feel I really want to pray she'll listen to sense, that she'll stop destroying herself, that she'll see how better life is when she's sober."

"Poor Pippy. You really want a lot. None of it may be possible. I've seen many a good guy go down with the disease, many a nice woman. It's a tricky old number."

I felt like screaming, tearing my hair out. The thought that Aggie's survival was so uncertain was unbearable.

Andy tore over to the window.

"A car."

"Great. Maybe they're going Aggie's way."

"Depends who it is."

Someone who knew the way to the yard. The car stopped and the door opened.

"You try to wake Aggie. I'll see who it is," I said to Andy.

A bronzed face smiled at me. Eddie.

"Just thought I'd call on the way back from the airport. Nothing like a holiday to make you glad you live in Limerick."

"You enjoyed it?" I asked, mentally clawing Clara to pieces.

"I wouldn't put it quite like that. It's just that you realise how well off you are."

I sat him down and put the kettle on, wondering what I would cook for lunch. He would need something if he was going back to Dublin.

"We're having lunch shortly – this is Andy," I gestured to the figure coming into the room.

I could see that Eddie was jumping to conclusions.

"My brother."

He shook hands warmly. Strange how our friendliness is contingent on what's in it for ourselves.

They chatted intensely about bones and aborigines and more bones. I rustled together a decent repast of pâté, vol-au-vent and cheesecake. No wine as he would be carrying a precious cargo.

I made strong coffee for Agatha and brought it in here to her. She was sitting upright but looked like death.

"Here, Ag. Try to swallow some of this. If you drink it all, I'll let you have a glass of wine."

It was gone in next to no time but I held back on the wine, pretended I couldn't find it.

"Brandy would do," her poor, sunken eyes pleaded.

"Not a chance, Ag. It would finish you off. I'll get some more coffee." The look on her face said she wouldn't touch it.

Back in the kitchen, the lunch went down a treat.

"You lucky fellow, having a sister to cook such delicious meals. A fellow could move mountains with that stuck to his ribs."

"Would you be up to moving a fairly small one, Eddie?"

He smiled.

"I'm afraid it would mean retracing your steps but you could stay here on your way back and join us for breakfast — or whatever you like."

"I'm too much of a gentleman to enforce my desires, especially when I've just survived unwelcome advances myself. Some people are great to look at but that's a far cry from wanting to get more friendly."

I presumed he was talking about Clara.

"You're just hidebound by your culture, old fella. The Abos wouldn't stand on ceremony. Whoever wants it generally gets it."

"Maybe my hormones need a boost or perhaps breast-feeding was a smothering experience. Anyway, you want me to do something, Pippy, I mean, Philippa."

"It's my sister. She needs to see a doctor. If you would promise to bring her to St Brendan's, I would be very grateful."

"All your rich food gone to her head?"

"I'm afraid it's serious. She's had several gallons of alcohol and a teaspoon of food for the past few days."

I put some cushions into the car and my spare duvet. Andy packed the case and put it in the boot. Eddie went into the sitting-room and sat with Aggie before they set off. As he turned towards me I could see he was affected. He shook his head as if he couldn't believe what he was seeing.

"I'll bring her out to the car if you would open the door. Maybe you'd give her a hot-water bottle too. She's very weak."

"Yes, I've already thought of that."

Slowly and gently, as if she would break, Eddie gathered Agatha's thin little body into his arms and carried her out of the room. Her head lolled to one side like that of a broken doll. He tucked her into the duvet with the concern of a worried parent and got into the car himself. I knew then she couldn't be in better hands. Bones were his whole life.

"Well, Sis. He seems like a good sort," Andy said, attempting some comfort.

"I've no doubt about that, Andy. None at all."

"You really expect me to believe that, Philippa!" Emily said, striding into the kitchen. "First Gaye Greene with a 'schoolfriend of Dickie's' and now you with your brother! I'll have to find myself an uncle or something. It seems to be the fashion at the moment. Clara seems to be the only person with a *bona fide* boyfriend."

"You mean Eddie?" I asked.

"No. He seems more interested in the dead, according to Clara. This fellow has one of those foreign-sounding names."

So, Eddie was definitely safe. Not even a 38" Cup D could do its worst.

"If Andy is your brother," Emily said slowly, "then who is Gerald?"

"Ah, who indeed. I'm still trying to discover."

"You mean, he's the one, the real boyfriend. So Andy is really . . . Gosh, I was so rude to him."

"Don't worry, he wouldn't notice. He's spent a lot of time in Australia."

"Tell me all about him. This isn't the one you met on Aran that Seamus talked about, is it?"

"Would you like some tea, Emily? How are Dickie's onions?"

Fortunately, there are some things Emily needs to talk about. I prefer to listen rather than reveal. Before you know where you are, you find yourself blurting out things you're better off keeping under wraps.

"They're about the size of a pinhead at the moment with one long green stalk. He was cossetting them in a propagator on top of a radiator. I told him too much warmth would dehydrate them and they'd shrivel up and die. You'd think I was telling him they'd catch the plague. He went straight out and bought a misting unit. So now they're bathing in tropical warmth. They grow at least an inch a day. I daren't ask but I have a squint at the chart when he's at work. The number of times I've lifted the lid with a scissors in my hand."

"But you restrained yourself."

"Only just. I thought marrows were bad but these are infinitely worse. Not even a nice flower to look at and something to eat at the end of it. I have no intention of eating these monsters. I'd be ill."

We poured the tea and I shared my tin of caramel slices. Emily only ever takes one.

"Sorry to hear about Nanny. If I'd known I'd have come to say good-bye but Clara only told me yesterday."

Eddie and his big mouth. Going all the way to Morocco to talk about Nanny and me.

"The other thing she talked about was the proposed trip in the summer. She feels the south of France would be ideal. It's got Celtic remains, the Camargue with its black cattle that are like the Irish Dexter, it's coming down with flowers and the wine is good."

"Of course, Seamus doesn't like wine but he needn't come. What about Dickie and his onions? And Gaye Greene and the baby, I suppose Mr Greene could look after it."

"It's not due until July. Of course, we don't know what it's like there. Could be quite dangerous. They say all the white slave trade goes through Marseilles and on to the Middle East."

"I think, Emily, we are all fairly safe from ending up in the arms of a rich Arab. They prefer them young and plump. Clara will presumably have her boyfriend to protect her. Morocco is only a stone's throw away from Provence when you're in love."

"We'll have to put it to a vote."

I didn't bother putting bets on the outcome.

The postman brought a letter from Agatha. Nothing from Gerald. A parcel for Andy. He obviously thinks he has taken up residence.

I had a cup of tea and caramel slice before tackling Aggie's torture. Little did she realise that however bad it was for her, it was just as bad watching, unable to do anything.

Dear Pips, it began. Always an ominous beginning.

Please come and get me out of here it's full of people with half a brain raving mad, shouting and banging around so you can't get a wink of sleep. If only I could sleep everything would be all right. They've given me pills but they don't work. I begged Eddie not to leave me but he said he'd be back when I was better. He comes every day now. You'd think he'd have something better to do.

How is Andy? I had a lovely dream about Australia. Maybe if I went back with him things would be better I could get a nice job and a house near the sea or maybe in the bush. Andy says it's really nice far from so-called civilisation. The psychiatrist here says I'm suffering from alienation, the modern disease where we feel dislocated. He gave me a book to read, all about suffering. I don't need any more of that. See you soon. Love and kisses to Andy.

Ag

PS Why did you have to do this to me?

Same old story. Ag's illness had nothing to do with what she was doing to herself. She was too ill to see Eddie's kindness for what it was. She'd be out in days, none the wiser, just cross at me for doing something she thought was totally unnecessary. I wished I was good at praying.

The door opened. "Everything seems to be a-blooming out there," Andy announced. "Little white things, some kind of orchid and what looks like the faint beginnings of bluebell leaves thrusting their little spikes into the air."

Gerald said he'd come in bluebell time.

"You look a bit down in the dumps. Let's crack a couple of tubes of beer," Andy said, manoeuvring a basket of wood through the door and closing it with his foot.

I wish he had more respect for the paintwork. It's not your log cabin in the bush.

"Beer is the last thing on my mind. I've just had a letter from Agatha."

"Ah."

He filled the range with neatly chopped logs and put the kettle on.

"Maybe a cuppa."

He took the cups from the dresser.

"You really care about her, don't you? Lots of people would have given up long ago," he said, putting my cup and saucer before me.

"I wish I didn't care so much. It's as if someone is pulling out my insides bit by bit."

"A bit dramatic, old Sis. Tell her to go to hell if it's that bad. It's up to her in the end."

"I know that. It doesn't make it any easier. Parcel for you."

He lifted it from the table and examined it carefully.

"It might be easier to open it," I suggested but he wasn't listening. He smelt it, shook it and rubbed his fingers up and down it.

I handed him a knife. He looked at me in horror and shook his head.

"No sense in all this shilly-shallying. Open the darn thing."

"This is too important to rush. Just be quiet."

Stung into silence, I got up from the table. Better to be doing something useful than sit and listen to abuse. The sooner he went back to Australia, the better.

"Happy Christmas, Sis," Andy said, dangling a wooden shape in front of my eyes. "Sorry it arrived a bit late. Had a mate send it over fast as he could." I took it from him. A primitive carving in the round with staring eyes and legs apart.

"Not a Sheela-na-Gig! They have them over there too?"

"Female power is a very strong part of Aboriginal culture and that little lady has the whole power of the tribe in her. All the feminists wear this little ornament. Got it specially. Thought it would suit you."

I could wear it around my neck and frighten Seamus away. On second thoughts, perhaps Sophia . . .

"I love it. I'll always treasure it. Over here they hide the figures away in museum basements. Women think it debases them when it really lets them see how powerful they are." I put it on. "You know, Andy, it's your second present to me. The first was when you were about ten you bought me a goldfish because its eyes reminded you of me."

"Obnoxious little turd I must have been. Can't remember much. Mother seemed to be always whining and the old man seemed to shout and lash out all the time."

"Can't say I want to think too much about it." I immediately thought of Agatha and wondered how she was. If only, if only.

"Agatha wants to go to Australia with you. She thinks a change would be just the thing."

"No way. She wouldn't last five minutes in the bush. You need all your wits about you there or you're dingo meat. You'd last, though. You've got staying power."

Will I stick it out though without tearing Gerald's clothes off when he comes? Perhaps the scent of bluebells will send him reeling.

"Eddie's been very good to Aggie. Been to see her every day. Maybe she'll listen to him. It's often from the strangest quarters we get most inspiration."

"Makes you wonder what he gets out of it, all the same. It's not as if Ag's anything to look at these days. Just skin and bone."

Quite.

February is the month of death. When we decide to die, apparently it's more likely to be in February, caught between the post-Christmas dip and pre-spring rise. PJ has been in, telling me about his new lambs, how many were still-born, how many the fox got and finally those who succumbed to E. coli. He's demented.

"The place has been in the family for six generations. They survived the famine, living on tree bark, turnips and frogs. The French think they invented them. My Da remembers the taste."

An idea perhaps for *Philippa's Pantry*, macedoine of frogs' legs, turnip and hawthorn. The prospects would probably go mad for it. I would make my fortune. But money isn't everything, though it's a lot.

"Do ye know, Miss Woodcock," PJ went on while, as usual, pieces of mud fell from his boots onto my quarry tiles, "I have a hankering for a flat with an entrance that isn't clogged with boots and dogs and fishing gear. Somewhere you press a switch and the heating is turned on without having to rake a fire through and coax it into a glow and spend your weekends sawing wood so you'll have hot water. A place where you can go to a freezer and take out one of them pies you buy in Marks & Spencers and stick it in a microwave oven and in seconds you have something that'll fill your belly. Somewhere you can sit down when you've a mind to and watch the telly or read the paper without the thoughts of having to go out and check on a cow calving or worry about a sick lamb. When you go home in the evening you know that's that, there won't be cattle breaking out or hay being rained on or silage going mouldy because it's too wet. What do you think of that now? Wouldn't that be a grand life?"

"It sounds damn boring to me, PJ. What about those cows you bought as heifers and reared them up to be fine Aberdeens that win at shows? What about those market days when you bring the calves and get the best price going because you've the best calves in the Midlands? What about the taste of fresh vegetables from your garden, the smell of the hay on a dark winter morning and the sound of animals grinding it between their teeth? The first primroses, the hazel catkins in January, the smell of the badger in the wood."

"If you go on like that, you'll have me in tears. Them are things I'd miss all right. But I'm not getting any younger. The young lad isn't interested in farming. He'd prefer to sell shirts and ties in Ballinamore and have his own car, three weeks holidays and off all weekend cavorting."

There are no answers, especially in February. The darkness has to have its turn, so that lightness can displace it. I made tea for PJ and offered him one of my caramel slices. I must have been feeling generous.

"You, now, Miss Woodcock, have it in an ideal way. No one to please but yourself. Your little bit of a business, your gaggle of friends and I heard tell at the party you're all off to the south of France for a few weeks. An ideal sort of life."

159

Indeed. I would have to think about that.

"I often thought," he went on waxing lyrical, "I'd like to sit in one of them cafés on the footpaths and just sit and watch people pass by and a glass of beer in your hand and the sun warming your back. But with cows to look after and hay to make and an empty pocket, it's more likely to be Bettystown I'll see."

"Don't worry, PJ," I reassured, "holidays are not what they're cracked up to be. The problem is we take our old selves with us and have to live with it for a few weeks without the distractions of work. Can be purgatory writ large."

I could see he didn't believe a word I said. Just try it, PJ. Just give it a try.

I was well advanced for spring with the potatoes in their sprouting trays. The tomato seeds were in the propagator, along with the courgettes – though I feel these are as overrated as Kiwi fruit and just as tasteless. However, the flower is pretty and the leaves large enough to suppress the weeds. The slugs were busy attacking the first shoots of anything that appeared above ground, particularly the delphinium. I rooted out the beer traps and got a gallon of dregs from Doolan's in the village. They don't believe for a minute I use it to turn the slugs into suicidal maniacs. I think they believe I drink it myself or use it to give my pâté that *je ne sais quoi*. People are crazy.

A Valentine card. Anonymous but it smelt of Gerald. A single red rose entwined with hearts.

" . . . A jug of wine, a loaf of bread – and thou . . . "

The thought of it made my head spin. Nothing would be more perfect. Alas, this life is mainly suffering, an opportunity to gain karma for the one to come. Though there's nothing to say it can't be obtained in a bluebell wood with a bottle of St Emilion. However, all this

Valentine business is such nonsense, a teenage thing. I remember the many cards I sent in the hope that some luckless fool would recognise my mini-skirt and long hair on the bus and know I was the one for him, though I wasn't quite as deluded as some. Patti Plunkett used to walk past her hero's house daily, which was quite out of her way, in the hope of catching a glimpse of him. What that would do for her I never discovered. Women are such silly creatures, bestowing all their energy on a male who doesn't even know they're alive and even if he does, women are just handy to hold onto when the going gets rough or they've got an itch to scratch. As Léon said of Emma Borary, "How to get rid of her afterwards is the problem." Some women expect more. Only some. In the south of France making love was an end in itself, nothing before or after. Quite as it should be. Love itself is another thing.

"It's all been settled, Philippa, the trip to France," Gaye Greene called to inform me. "We're to bring our partners. How about you bringing that nice man who was at the Christmas party? I didn't get talking to him." She settled into the large armchair as I poured the tea.

"I doubt if it's Gerald's cup of tea," I hastily replied, opening my tin of caramel slices. Only three left. This was touching rock bottom. Andy would have to go.

"But you'll come yourself – we're all going."

By "all" I presume she meant Dunkie Doodle Dandy too. How cosy.

"I suppose I will. Andy will be here to hold the fort. He knows all about planting vegetables and looking after animals, so I'll be able to indulge myself for once. I think I'm quite looking forward to getting away."

"So are we. The baby isn't due until July. Emily and Clara have everything more or less arranged. Emily's dying to get away. The smell of onion is driving her crazy. We're all to attend the AGM on the tenth to get everything sorted out. So be sure to come."

If my courage didn't fail me in the meantime.

"Clara is very anxious to see Mo – short for Mohammed – again. He's been writing every day. She showed me one of his letters. Quite passionate. Talks endlessly about her 'beautiful titties'."

It figures. Arrested at the weaning stage. She'll never be

allowed to breast-feed. The jealousy would be too much for him to bear. Another poor baby with a pot belly and an allergy to cheese.

I poured us some more tea and the last of the caramel slices disappeared into Gaye's bulge.

"They're so good, Philippa, I must order a few dozen from you. Dunkie is still talking about the wonderful food you had at the party. Not at all like the spread at Sophia's, though it's naughty of me to discuss someone else's hospitality."

"Oh, I can stand a little bitching now and again."

"Well, there were two bottles of champagne between all of us. Seamus got the giant's share and Clara a close second. Teresa and Dotty settled for tea, like PJ's wife. PJ himself went home and brought back a bottle of Black Bush. That did the damage. Everyone began to shout and get a bit cross with one another."

The things you miss when you're bent on seduction.

"That sounds exciting," I encouraged.

"Well, Sophia was doing her best to instill a bit of culture into deaf ears. She brought out several copies of her book and was giving it away at bargain prices. Not a sinner would buy it. I didn't because I don't know the first thing about painting. Dunkie would have bought one, except Dickie put him off it, telling him he could buy heating cables for the same amount of money. Seamus was mad keen for one when he saw the nude pictures."

"What had they to do with 'climate and the artist'?"

"According to Sophia, you only ever get nude painting in warm climates. Models won't pose in the freezing cold."

Simple. It probably took a mountainside of trees so that such a startling contribution could be made to our knowledge.

"The men all had a ball. They retired to Robert's hobby room where he has his train set and computer. Dunkie couldn't tear himself away from Duke Nukum and Percy and Dickie were of course enthralled with the train set. They ran it round and round, changed signals, stopped at stations to load up imaginary water and coal. What they get from it all beats me. I'd rather watch a flower open. I had to pretend indigestion before I could budge them. It was two when we got to bed. We've all been invited back for a re-run. Probably the night I'm going badger-watching."

"I thought you enjoyed a little get-together, Gaye."

"To be honest, the only thing I enjoy at the moment is thinking about the baby coming. We've everything more or less ready. Dunkie made the cleverest little cradle carved with sprays of macrocarpa at either end, to remind us how it all began."

I could think of other ways but I simply said, "That must be nice," trying to hide the fear in my voice. So much to go wrong.

As I washed the dishes later, I realised my pleasures were confined to smelling the fresh blooms of gorse and watching Nanny's kids grow. Where were Gerald or Andy or Agatha in any of it? Makes one wonder about human relationships and the pleasure one derives from them.

"Phone, Pips," Andy shouted.

"You take it." I had no inclination for even semi-human contact. I slipped out and walked as far as the biggest tree on the farm. A giant sycamore growing from the ruins of a cabin. The shape of its well still there, though filled in with cart-loads of stones. Why did they build there, on a tiny scrap of land far from any road? Was the woman pregnant, caught in the purple heather on a hot day in autumn with an insistent and eager male pulling at her clothes and achieving his aim? Their little pathway barely visible, a dark green ridge in the grass and on either side the shadows of potato ridges and just like my little barely formed baby, gone into the earth, as crumbs are washed clean from plates.

I arrived back and found a message. "Ag rang to say she's out and Eddie is bringing her down to Limerick. He thinks a change of scene might help her."

Poor deluded fool.

I arrived at Claffey's on the tenth for the AGM. The air was buzzing with excitement, pieces of paper flying everywhere, brochures and language cassettes.

"You parlay fransay, don't you, Philippa?" said Clara accusingly from behind a brochure on the sun-spots of the Côte d'Azur, her tan looking remarkably fresh.

"Don't mind her," Noreen whispered to me from behind a large G & T. "She's mad keen to speak the lingo. She doesn't know the first thing about this Arab she's met and she wants to quiz him up and down. He could be a date picker for all she knows. Seamus says what does it matter, can't they use body language."

"Is Seamus coming to Provence?" I asked.

"He can't wait to see the wall-to-wall flesh he's been hearing about. Bought himself a special pair of sunglasses with the mirror on the outside so you can't tell where he's looking. Men have only one thing on their minds. I wouldn't mind if he was a ball of fire himself. Far from it."

A little early in the evening for such revelations, I felt. Beggars can't be choosers. Such morsels were welcome any time. They make one feel that however bad our own life is, someone else's is infinitely worse.

Emily got the ball rolling and informed us of the itinerary. We were to leave at 7.30 am for Paris where we would pick up a plane to Nice. After a week or so there, we would catch the train for Aix-en-Provence where her second cousin, once removed, had booked us all into the University Residence.

"Each day has something arranged," Emily went on.

"You don't have to go, of course. But these tours are very good value. You are advised to bring tea bags, a decent pair of walking shoes and plenty of money."

Despite misgivings, I was excited at the prospect. The thought of seeing once more the haze of spring on the hills of Provence and smell the heat of the red clay cheered me up. Very un-Buddha-like. One should be neither up nor down. And of course, the rosé is like nectar.

No sooner had the first bluebell shone forth than Gerald arrived. I barely had time to comb my hair and put on my bra.

He looked tired and sad.

"Anything wrong?" I asked, surprised to see him in such obvious lack of command.

"Nothing's right. But at least I'm here, to breathe a short breath of fresh air."

We sat by the fire Andy had built up and then tactfully found he had something to collect in Ballinamore.

"What would you like – tea, coffee, brandy?"

"To be honest, I don't know. Well, perhaps some of your excellent pâté on your wholesome brown bread and a slight glass of wine."

It would have to be a special Chablis I had hidden under the stairs for an emergency.

When I came back with it all, he was asleep. His soft eyes closed, his full lips barely open taking in long, easy breaths. His shoes looked tight on his feet. I gently undid the laces. His hand touched my head in thanks and he was out for the count. I ate the bread and pâté and drank more of the wine than I should have. By the time he woke up, it was pitch dark. Bedtime.

Andy and I were talking in the kitchen.

"Sorry," Gerald said, embarrassed. "I'd no idea you had company."

"I'm just a hanger-on, Gerry. The no-good brother."

"Gerry" was as bad as "Pippy". I would have to take Andy aside later.

"You'll be feeling peckish," I said, to save Gerald having to reply.

"Very. My abject apologies for conking out like that. Unforgivable."

"On the contrary. I'm flattered you felt relaxed enough to do it here."

I felt Andy shift about a bit.

"Well, I'll go and crash out. See you in the morning."

The silence of the night was with us. The kettle hissing on the range, the clock ticking, the click of my shoes on the floors.

"Really good to be here. I've had a traumatic time. Someone is about to sue me for libel. They're saying I wrote about them in my latest book. I never met them in my life before! But how do you prove that? Then my sister is doing her best to torment me, saying I should be spending more time with Father and I should use a pseudonym as I'm an embarrassment to her. To cap it all, my cat died. I think that was the worst thing that happened."

I have seen grown men cry and Gerald was close to tears. It was good to know his feelings were still intact . . .

I took his hand and held it to my cheek.

"That's really hard luck, Gerald. Trouble always comes in bursts, when we're least expecting it and least able for it."

He leaned forward and kissed me softly on the lips.

"I knew you would understand. I just knew it. It's nice to be right, for once."

After that, we got on like a house on fire. Far from pulling back, like most men do, as if revealing vulnerability was not manly, Gerald grew happier in our cosy intimacy.

167

Of course it was meat and drink to me, parched in an emotional wasteland.

When the supper dishes were washed, I led him to the pink room once more, slyly knocking the phone off the hook as I went.

I lingered in the room, sat on the bed, put on the bedside lamp, turned out the main one, switched on some music and tried to look as soft and inviting as I could.

Within minutes, we were lying beside each other on the pillow, chatting away, tucking the duvet up around our still-clothed bodies trying to get warm. We were soon sound asleep. Obviously I'm not a single-minded seductress – or else a very poor one. Trouble is, with Gerald I feel so relaxed and trusting. It plays havoc with one's baser instincts.

I awoke to the sound of the music tape having reached its limit, slipped out of bed and went to my chaste couch. Perhaps I'd have more luck amongst the bluebells.

"Something about the air round here renders me comatose. I feel so relaxed," Gerald said as he poured hot water into the teapot.

I had taken out my silver one – EPNS of course, but very handsome nonetheless.

"The Midlanders say it's because we're in a basin with the mountains around the coast and the air is stale. I invite them to come across the bog with me and let them feel it whip the skin from their bones. Perhaps you need a holiday, overdoing it."

"Writing is no penance to me. It's like earning your living from your favourite hobby, child's play. Perhaps I haven't recovered from the family spirit at Christmas. When I'm just about getting over it, the next will be on top of me."

"You really should tell that sister of yours where to get

off. And your father should stand up for you a bit more."

"Well, Philippa, it's great to offer someone else advice on how to fix their family problems but it's the easier option. Much more difficult to do when it's your own problem. Probably because you're part of the problem too. Well conditioned."

I felt like not giving him any breakfast. He has a nerve to think his problems are similar to mine. They're infinitely worse.

Andy came quietly through the kitchen and out the back door. He obviously thought there was a "scene". He needn't have worried. I'm not given to hysterics – at least nothing very obvious.

We let the ducks out, fed the kids and went to check on the pigs and sheep. Poppy and her calf had found a sunny corner and lay side by side, chewing the cud and watching us with their big, vacant eyes. The sheep bleated at us for some food and ran away when they saw they were getting nothing.

"We'll bring them some hay tomorrow, otherwise they won't finish up what they have left. They're so fussy. When someone else has it, like Poppy, it's the tastiest morsel around and worth stealing."

In the distance the trees stood lacy with fresh new leaves and alive with birdsong. When all the nests were built and eggs laid, the cuckoo would come and perform his con trick, like Dunkie.

Gerald put an arm on my shoulder.

"Let's go and see these bluebells," he said.

"Yes, let's. The pigs can wait."

My knees went to jelly. When it came to the crunch, I was lily-livered, not the brave, sultry temptress of my fantasy.

Blues and mauves splashed through the wood like a shimmering canvas by Monet.

Gerald stood and looked.

"We daren't walk on them," he whispered, bending to touch one.

"It's okay to walk on the flowers but the leaves are easily damaged. I suppose we could take our boots off," I said spiritedly, not meaning a word of it.

He soon found a dry log and sat and removed his boots. I was so glad to see he kept his socks on. If anything turns me off, it's the sight of a man's toenails.

"Better follow suit. Must humour the visitor."

"I hope I'm a little more than that," he said, taking my hand and folding it in his.

"A bit," I said, smiling. No need to make them feel they've conquered all.

"Ah, Pips. You're a funny character. Sometimes you give so wholeheartedly and sometimes you're tight as a tick."

"Where on earth did you hear such an expression, as if I were some sort of bloodsucker."

"Now don't take offence. I don't mean it like that. And even if I did, it's part of you, so I . . . I like it very much."

Something melted inside my heart. I bent my head and kissed him with more feeling than I thought was safe to admit to. I needn't have worried. His response was even greater. Soon we reached that wonderful realisation by touch alone that we felt strongly about each other.

My hand slipped onto his belt and I had it open in seconds. How far is too far? I wasn't complaining but how was he? My fingers slid along the roundness of his tummy and paused. His hand slipped from my breast. He sat bolt upright.

"You sure you're warm enough?"

"Mmmmm," I murmured, "quite sure." I pulled him towards me again and lay down on the bluebells. Love can damage nothing. A bruised flower here or there is immaterial. I eased my belt and allowed my zip to unravel.

The smell of crushed bluebell was overpowering. Gerald picked one, feathered it across my lips and kissed me as he put it in my hair. He didn't seem to feel any urgency. I encouraged him as gently as I could and removed the remainder of the inhibiting clothes. The sun seemed as hot as summer and the smells as intense. If it weren't for the wet sap of bluebell on my bottom, it would have been glorious.

"Philippa," Gerald's voice said from somewhere far away. "I want to talk to you."

"Chat away," I said. It's always more interesting when the action has sound effects too.

Nothing happened, so I opened my eyes. The man looked positively miserable.

"What is it, Gerald? Don't worry, I've taken precautions."

"It's not that. It's . . . difficult to talk about. Perhaps I should have said it sooner. Perhaps I should never have come back."

I was intrigued. It's often the female who blurts out past misdemeanours, talks about the several children adopted in various parts of the world, how they put holes in their boyfriend's condoms in order to deliberately get pregnant to force him to stay.

"Well, you're here now. Can you not say what it is and then we can get on with enjoying ourselves."

"That's just it. It's to do with what's happening."

Married? Impotent? Or heaven forfend, AIDS?

"You said in Aran that you were a widower, that Mrs Ransome was dead."

"I was referring to my mother. I have never been married."

"I know – you prefer men."

"No, no. Nothing like that," he laughed.

He turned away from me. I wished he'd relieve my agony, my bum was freezing.

171

"The truth is, Pippy, I'm a virgin. I've never had . . . it."

Well, there are fewer things guaranteed to take a girl's breath away and make her put her clothes back on. It seemed immodest to be displaying oneself in front of an innocent.

"That's okay, Gerald," I managed gallantly, though feeling murderously disappointed.

"I thought it would just sort of happen," he said, running his fingers through his beautiful hair, "that I'd get so carried away, I would find the whole business over and done with before I knew what was going on."

"Problem is, Gerald, that the old head doesn't let us off the hook so lightly. The old saboteur is there, ready to pounce at the first step out of line. Or, perhaps you had second thoughts."

"About you – none whatever. You're the first person I have actually liked enough to even 'bare my soul', not to mention the rest of me," he said, rearranging his clothes.

So several bluebells had been bruised and damaged for nothing. We walked home for lunch, hand in hand. What seemed so amicable and civilised earlier was now clouded by a new awareness.

"We're making it seem like a tragedy, Gerald, when I should be feeling so flattered that you have chosen me as your first, em . . . "

"Yet that's not how you feel."

"I suppose, I'm disappointed. I was expecting something to happen and it didn't. But because I know the reason, it's easy enough to get over."

He put his arm on my shoulder and hugged me to him.

"It'll be okay. Everything will work out," he said, trying to reassure himself.

The phone was busier than ever. Andy usefully employed himself taking orders for *Philippa's Pantry* and increasing the price at the same time. No one quibbled. Instead of a mere 50%, I was now making 75%.

"Try some new things. You must get your R & D department really hard at it, Sis," Andy exhorted, "bringing out something new every six months."

Typical male attitude to business. They think if something is doing well now, then bigger and more will do even better. No point in telling him how wrong he is. He wouldn't believe me. He was brought up to think a man's opinion is more valuable than a woman's. It would take a brain transplant to disabuse him of that notion.

"I prefer to stick with what I have and do that well. After all, sales are increasing," I said firmly.

"But Sis . . . " he went on. Fortunately the phone rang again. I went back to making my umpteenth batch of Marmalade with Mead and wondered how Gerald was, back in his lonely bachelor pad with no cat and a libel suit hanging over his head.

In the midst of my musings, a car appeared in the yard, one of those old Morris Minors with wooden sides. This one had gleaming chrome and scrubbed tyres.

I put on my business face and went out.

Gloria, from the spinning course in Bath, climbed out.

"I promised I'd call. Me and Hank had a bit of a falling-out. So I chopped down all the apple trees and ran away."

"Was Hank not a bit cross with you?" Perhaps the police were hot on her heels.

"He did something even worse, so he won't be looking for me."

I shuddered to think what Hank's sin was and I didn't ask.

"Come in. Just in time for tea."

I popped two scones into the oven and put the kettle on the boil. Visitors never come when the house is spick and span and you've just baked a beautiful fruitcake. I supposed

173

Gloria would be staying, at least until Hank had finished clearing the orchard.

"Did you suddenly take a scunner to cider?"

"The first few gallons were okay, a bit sweet but okay. The next lot Hank insisted on adding some brandy he got cheap from a distillery where they were throwing out their old barrels. Maggoty, of course, and turned the whole lot into ditch-water. Even the pigs wouldn't touch it. Lost me rag then, I did. Lucky I didn't lop his head off."

Not to be trifled with, our Gloria. A "spirited gal", mother would have called her.

"Nice place you got here," she said, ladling marmalade on her scone as if it were going out of style.

"Lovely road up to it. All those bushes with white flowers and the nice stone walls."

The girl obviously needed watching. I hoped she'd left the chainsaw behind. One day a tree, the next a person. Who knows what makes someone snap?

"Did you have a difficult upbringing, Gloria?" The non-sequitur slipped out as I poured some more tea.

"You bet. Father a drunken lout. Used to break every dish in the 'ouse. Mum nutty about flowers, 'n animals and things."

For once I was pleased to have Andy staying. The local B & B should have a room for her at this time of year.

"Unfortunately, I haven't enough room at the moment," I began, breathing deeply. "I have my brother staying and my sister may return at a moment's notice. You're welcome to stay tonight on the couch but with an unmarried male in the house, I'm afraid if that should continue, it would be utterly condemned by the neighbours and my house shunned as a place of sin. The postman would tell all. Around here, he's the moral policeman."

During my little speech, Andy had sidled into the room, unnoticed. He gave me an odd look. For his own sake, I hoped he wouldn't make things difficult.

"This is Gloria, a friend from Bath. Just a short visit. She's looking for somewhere to stay, so I'll ring Flaherty's and book her in. How long will I tell them?"

"Not sure," she said, taking the pattern from the plate as her knife split the scone.

I went off, gulped a few breaths of air and phoned Flaherty's. I didn't mention the chainsaw. Anyway, they had droves of strong lads to fend her off if the lid flipped.

"Good news," I announced to an empty room. Through the window I saw Gloria and Andy in deep discussion over the engine of her car.

Cooking takes my mind off worries, so I began a complicated Indian recipe for lunch.

"She's not such a bad sort," Andy boomed, coming into the house and scaring the wits out of me.

"She's just killed an orchard of trees. I wouldn't bet on it."

"She just got mad. She's fine now. You know the feeling."

"Only too well but I restrain myself. The trees did nothing on her. They were simply minding their own business, producing cider apples for years and years and suddenly, without a by-your-leave, it's curtains. All because she got mad with someone else."

"Suppose it could have been a person she lopped but didn't."

"That's precisely my point. We know not the time nor the hour."

"Aw, Sis, you're a bit of an exaggerator. She wouldn't hurt a fly."

I had momentarily forgotten that Andy had lived in the bush for years. If he knew the world as I did, he would understand.

Two days later, Gloria was still sleeping on the couch and eating me out of house and home. I was at the end of my tether. On the third day, I left the house early and took the train to Dublin to cheer myself up.

Crossing the Liffey from Heuston Station, smelling the old smells and watching the seagulls peck at the green sludge is like not so much a home-coming as a going back. It's as if my little farm is far away, locked into the future, while Dublin is the past. I wouldn't wish these sad, painful feelings on anyone, except perhaps Gloria.

I usually visit Mother's grave, wedged between a tall statue of an angel and a long slab of polished stone topped by an urn. Hers is a length of granite, hard but with tiny specks of brightness. I chat away to her, tell her what I've been up to, though as usual she's not particularly interested but at least I have her immobilised. I cast a single red rose onto the grey stone and say goodbye. Father's grave is on the west coast, near Roundstone, looking towards the New World. He died on the banks of the Corrib, fishing for salmon. We hadn't the heart to take him from where he was happiest.

I sent a card to Gerald, a simple one with a bunch of violets. *Thinking about you. Hope the work is going well. Best regards.* Nothing very exciting, just a word of encouragement in case he needed it. His revelation still floored me. I had always assumed that knowledge of sex was an occupational hazard for men, that it came with the territory.

And of course, I always visited Nellie, Mother's old housekeeper or "woman" as she infuriatingly referred to her. She lived in the basement flat in a house in Marlborough Road. The wallpaper had big, red cabbage roses and green trelliswork, the floors covered in plain carpets, and the chairs were festooned with antimacassars. Brass gleamed everywhere.

"A brass for Nellie," was our demand on the last day of our seaside holidays.

"I was just after thinking about you, Apple of my Eye," said Nellie, greeting me with one of her pet names for me, all derived from Pip.

Once inside the door of Nellie's flat, you were home, except for a bedroom with a shower in one corner.

"Economical on movement" was how she described the lack of space. Nellie never complained. Took everything as it was.

"You look a bit peaky," she said, ushering me to a chair. "Overdoing the lambing or calving? No man, that's your trouble. He'd make you take it easy. Give you a baby, so you'd be stuck in a chair breast-feeding."

"No fear of that, Nellie. The most likely man for a long time turns out to be a total beginner. A virgin. Have you ever heard of a man not knowing what to do?"

There were no holds barred with Nellie. I always told her everything, like it was.

"Well, I suppose I could have but I didn't, if you underfollow me. I knew precious little myself, so they could have been doing it back to front for all I knew. Come to think of it, in those days we never talked about it much, except for a few scare stories at school. One was about a woman who went to the doctor to see why she couldn't have a baby. When the doctor took a look, he found her naval in shreds. Turns out her husband thought that's where to put it."

"Well, Gerald knows roughly how it's supposed to be but seems to be frightened of something. Which makes me feel terrified, needless to say. What if he hates it if he has it with me?"

"Well, that'll be up to him. We all make our own pleasure. In these things a bit of affection counts for a lot. Think how lucky you are – you don't run any risk of some foul disease or nits."

"Crabs, Nellie. Nits are the things you get in your hair."

"Sure, aren't they my best friends. Many's the one you brought home from school."

She poured her black tea from the Country Rose teapot into the tiny china cup. Nellie's tea is special. You can feel it doing you good. A case of "Better a dish of herbs where love is than a stalled ox and hatred therewith."

"Now, tell me. How is that brother of yours? An awkward little devil when he was a child. But then your father was very hard on him."

"Yes, I can remember some of it. He was a bit of a boor to begin with but settled down eventually. In fact, everything was going fine until Gloria turned up. Unfortunately, during one of my more generous moments, I was silly enough to give Gloria my address. She seemed so keen on spinning and cider and Hank, it seemed a safe bet she wouldn't come. Now she's ensconced in my living room, eating all my caramel slices and trying to ingratiate herself with Andy. I don't know which is worst. She terrifies me. She just murdered an orchard of apple trees without remorse."

"Not the best recommendation," said Nellie, stoking the fire and placing more lumps of black coal wherever she could find a space.

"Trouble is, I think Andy likes her. We were getting on so well, too."

Nellie passed the apple tart with cream and filled my cup.

"Poor old Ag is still ill, I may as well tell you."

"I thought as much, though I pray for her every night. Drink is what has the country ruined. What's to become of her?"

"There's a slight glimmer of hope. She's got a friend, at last. She couldn't have asked for anyone nicer. Eddie Henderson, the archaeologist. You remember me bringing him home?"

"Yes. And your Mother telling him her seed, breed and generation. Huguenots fleeing persecution. Artists in lace and linen. She could be a bit trying, your Mother."

"Eddie was so nice about it all. Listened so politely and never grumbled. He used to say she was the saddest person he ever met.

The fire hissed away and the big grandfather clock ticked to its heart's content. Through the lacy curtains we watched the legs of people going past, their arms straining with plastic bags, or children. I could have stayed forever, merely an onlooker not the driver of life's bus.

I woke to the sound of activity in the "kitchen." A pair of boiled eggs sat snug in woollen cosies with thickly buttered brown bread at their sides.

"This'll perk you up. You look a lot better than when you came. Don't worry, you haven't missed your train. Another two hours."

Nellie knew me inside out. I sank back and relaxed.

"Tell me all about this holiday. You didn't say much on the phone. Froggieland, isn't it? Knew a Frenchman once. Lovely moustache but terrible BO."

"Yes, we're going on the fifteenth for a fortnight. The entire Archaeological Society."

"That won't cause any traffic jams . . . "

"Well, including next of kin. I plan to spend as much time as possible away from them. Can't think why I'm going in the first place."

"Because you need a holiday. You're overdoing it with all these potted things and animals."

"You must come down again to see them, Nellie. You'd love Poppy's calf and the twins Nanny left. And I've triplet lambs."

"Thanks all the same. All that greenery is disorientating when you're used to bricks and mortar. And the fresh air is a killer. Took me weeks to recover from the last time."

"I promise next time to let you sit by the fire. No walks or visits to the village. It'll be just like home."

"Well, I might consider. Wait till the arthritis season is finished."

As soon as I saw Andy's bulk at the station, I knew something was up. I was tempted to stay on the train but stopped myself. After all, it might be something good, like Gloria got homesick or Agatha got the pioneer pin.

I just looked at him.

"Now don't just react, Sis. It's both good and bad."

I knew it. The train doors were still open. As if reading my mind, he grabbed my arm and steered me towards the van with *Philippa's Pantry* in pink and grey calligraphy.

"One of the pigs began farrowing," he began in his "I'm telling it like it happened" voice, the sort of tone he used with Mother when it turned out he'd been trying to steal apples on his way home from school.

"Glorry and I decided . . ."

"Glorry" indeed. When someone allows themselves to be called that, they must be determined . . .

"Are you listening?" I gave him my best stare.

"Well, we thought it would be best if we brought her in, ye know, in case the infra-red was needed."

"The reason I got outdoor pigs in the first place, Andrew, was to save all this 'mollycoddling' that you're so fond of criticising." I thought it prudent to let him see he was on a loser from the start.

"Okay, maybe we used our initiative when we shouldn't. Anyway, no sooner had we got the pig to the shed than she started. Out they came, one after another like beans spilling from a tin."

"I didn't know you were a poet too."

That did it. He was quiet for at least ten seconds.

However, once inside the car, he took it up again but

with a little less enthusiasm. Dreadful to have such power over someone.

"As soon as the last one was out Glorry and me had bets . . . "

I froze him with a stare.

"What I mean is, I took up the fork to arrange the straw and strike me dead if I didn't spear one of the little bastards with it."

It sounded a bit too pat.

"Was Glorry very upset at what she'd done?" I asked quietly.

"In bloody bits, she hadn't meant to . . . you bloody tricked me! I was going to take all the blame. She didn't mean any harm, Sis. She was just trying to round them up and get 'em all sucking so they wouldn't die and my God the little idiot walked straight onto the fork."

"The sun in the bush obviously bleached your grey cells. No one but an arboricidal maniac would round up a herd of bonhams with a fork! And you're prepared to forgive her, to blame the poor animal for wandering about breathing its first breath! You're the sort of person who goes soft on criminals, who says the father who abuses his own daughter was 'under pressure' or 'an alcoholic'. You don't really believe in punishment for wrongdoing because you've gone soft on yourself!"

"You just have it in for Gloria. Nothing she can do will change that. Your mind-set is fixed."

"I look at the evidence before me and so far we have one dead orchard and one . . . it is dead?"

"Not very happy anyway."

Only one thing worse than death and that's a slow one.

When we got to the farm, I ran to see the poor thing. It was lying flat out, eyes closed, barely breathing, drained of blood through the gash in its leg. I gathered it up, put it in the van and brought it to the vet. Perhaps when he saw it suffering he would put it out of its misery. Gloria wisely was nowhere to be seen.

The trip to Provence was definitely out of the question. By the time I returned, every animal in the place would be murdered.

As soon as the piglet was out of its misery, I told Emily.

"But you can't call it off at this stage, Philippa. You've paid your deposit and you won't get it back," she said sonorously.

"I don't care about the money; I'd rather have my farm intact."

"But we would miss you."

"Don't be silly. You'll have Sophia." I couldn't resist the little dig.

"Everyone thinks we're thick as thieves. It's just that no one else really understands her."

We probably understand her only too well but, as usual, I kept my mouth shut.

The weather promised to be dry for the foreseeable future so I decided to make the silage. It had to be cut, left to wilt and then gathered, rolled into a bale and covered in black clingfilm. The advantage was the lack of waste and also, the chances of having all of them go off were slim, whereas with a silage clamp any rot could spread through the whole clamp, not to mention being environmentally unfriendly with its leaching poisons.

The silage makers had to be fed and half the potato patch and much of my spare stores went in fodder. It was like throwing buns to bears. They obviously never got a decent meal in their lives. Andy was busy singing my praises to get back into my good books and procured a few orders for ducks and pâté. He was wasting his time.

As soon as the silage was baled, a young lad came along with a pair of metal arms hitched to the front of the tractor and put them in neat rows. Andy proceeded to spread some rock phosphate and we closed the field to let the grass grow a little before the sheep got onto it.

"Thank you for your help, Andrew," I said, a little stiffly.

"Think nothin' of it, Sis," he said, putting an unwelcome arm around me. "Ye know, it's too bad about what happened. I blame myself. Shouldn't have let Glorry have that fork. I thought she knew what she was doing."

I said nothing.

"What I mean is, I thought she knew how dangerous a fork is. She didn't mean to harm the little piggy. Honest."

"I believe you really believe that, Andy. But those trees she chopped. The evidence is stacked against her."

"Yeh, it looks kinda bad. But she's a good sort. Great at massage."

"I'm sure," was all I trusted myself to say.

"I don't mean anything . . . I mean, Sis, she gave my back a great rub," he shouted, as I headed for the house.

But he'd already lost me.

I kept myself busy. Idleness gives way to murderous thoughts. The remainder of the pigs farrowed without mishap. Where there were once three pigs there were now thirty-one screaming piglets and three very busy mothers with very red teats and appetites that were insatiable. No sooner were they fed one meal than they were looking for another.

I re-limed the goathouse for the winter, a satisfying job when all the dirt and scratches are covered up so easily. Would the same were true of people's characters. It's always those aspects of ourselves we least want to acknowledge that we dislike in other people. Was I murderous? Would I kill a tree, a pig? It was while I was doubting, during that brief window of opportunity for forgiveness, that Andy approached me.

"What's this I hear about you not going to Provence?

You know I'll look after everything. You can trust me."

"That is my dilemma, Andrew. I thought I could. I went away for a day to Dublin and I find a dead piglet on my return. It kind of threw me."

"Sure, in the light of what happened. But we've apologised. Glorry is still in bits about it. Has nightmares about pigs getting their revenge and eating her alive. She's lost over a stone in the past two weeks."

This was good news indeed.

"I don't really wish her any particular harm," I lied through my teeth. Not death anyway, just a little suffering.

"Well, I think she's been through enough," he said with a slight crackle in his voice I didn't like. "I'd really like you to get to know her better."

"These things cannot be forced. Wounds take time to heal," though the little piggy wasn't given much of a chance. "Don't forget, Andy, it was I who met Gloria first and I quite took to her. But I have learned that when the going gets rough, Gloria will run for cover."

I restrained myself from adding that this was a warning.

"Whatever about Gloria, I really want you to go on that holiday. You love France and need a break. I promise you I won't let Glorry next or near a four-legged friend while you're away."

"OK, I'll think about it," I said, sounding dubious but already packing my bags mentally.

There were the usual last-minute hitches, of course. Dickie Delaney had to arrange for someone to look after his onions. From a dozen applicants he selected a young lad from the village, on a flat rate plus a bonus if the onions put on growth while he was away. Emily said he was chosen because he was the only one who possessed a sleeping bag and a plethora of Boy Scout badges. He would need them in the polytunnel.

Noreen dropped her top set of teeth and had to have them repaired in a hurry. Gaye got the okay from the obstetrician and was ordered not to do too much sight-seeing. Poor Robert Dahling had an important contract to see to, which was only agreed at the eleventh hour. And of course, Dickie's pinstripe had to be taken from the cleaners. Couldn't go anywhere without that.

Gloria sent me a gift via Andy. A packet of Earl Grey tea. I find it hard to hold a grudge for long. Too soft.

Companions, like fish, go off after three days. We were in Nice, seated at Place Rossetti, in the old quarter, a magnificent square dominated by the Cathédrale of Ste Réparate. A favourite haunt of handbag snatchers. Sophia and Emily continued on the narrow road to the Castle while the more sensible of us admitted tiredness and decided on refreshments.

"Thank God we found it," said Noreen, nodding towards the church and swallowing her *citron pressé* with her lips drawn back at its unexpected sourness. "We know where to come for Mass."

She leaves nothing behind. Not even Seamus, who clings to her like a child would to a cuddly toy when its mummy is temporarily absent. I believe the man is frightened out of his wits with all the strangeness. The furthest he has been from home is Dublin and Lough Gur.

Teresa and Dotty complained about the tea, "yellow as dishwater", not the black treacle they're used to. They were warned to bring their tea bags but people seldom listen. They always think they know best.

My glass of burgundy tasted of fresh spring flowers. I ordered another. Dickie and Percy had a bottle of rosé between them. They seemed to be enjoying themselves, seated together at another table. Every time they laughed we looked, hoping they would share the joke. Of course, they were very wise.

Gaye and Dunkie were busy examining the window boxes with their avalanches of flowers and squealed with glee on being able to identify the wild flowers growing in the cracks beneath the tall apartment blocks. Gaye's child will be full of delight.

We were spared Clara and her beau for another few days. They were going to join us at Aix. Apparently Clara was paying Mo's boat fare from whatever hovel he crept in Morocco and would put him up at the University Residence. Love has no price.

I, on the other hand, watched an old women who peeked at us from behind her shutters. I caught her twice and warned the others to watch out for their handbags. The paint on her walls was flaking while that on the blue shutters was peeling like mad.

"You really must climb that hill, everyone. It's amazing. And there's a castle at the top." Sophia flopped into the spare chair at my table, spoiling my view of the cathedral.

"Here, Emily," she encouraged, pulling a chair from another table.

"Coffee for me, I'm afraid. I need to get a bit of energy for the descent," Sophia's teeth exploded onto whoever looked her way. Dare anyone say she wasn't having a whale of a time! I admired her scarf, an Isadora Duncan look-alike in raw silk, wrapped around her hair to protect it from the sun which would play havoc with that ash-blonde.

"Isn't this wonderful," she added, a trifle too earnestly.

I wondered where Dahling had got to but I didn't bother asking in case she thought I had the hots for her property.

"Well, I'll be a devil, seeing we're on holiday," Emily said coyly, "and get a carafe of the Provençal Rosé Philippa spoke about."

"Oh, be a bit more adventurous and have a kir. I'll join you after my coffee."

"Mixing coffee and alcohol is so bad for you," I said to no one in particular. "Apparently, the body doesn't know whether it's coming or going and gives up the ghost. Of course, perhaps you'd like to end your days in Nice, Sophia?" I asked with as much sincerity as I could muster.

"You're so *drôle*, Philly," she said. "So very *drôle*."

Like startled fawns Teresa and Dotty stopped chattering and sniffed at the air.

"Very quiet around here," Seamus said, waking up. "I prefer a bit of life myself. Best holiday we had was in Dublin. Plenty to do."

A pub on every street, full of Guinness.

"This is like the stuff that four-legged animals with manes do, not to put too fine a point on it," he said holding up his glass of beer.

"We understand your meaning perfectly, Seamus," Noreen said, "no need to embellish."

Seamus sat back sunken, holding his crotch as if in comfort. He reminded me of a child I knew who'd been sent to boarding school at five and never recovered. His hand was permanently in his pocket, massaging his member. Extraordinary. I wonder what women do for comfort?

"I think we should go to McDonald's for our dinner. I don't fancy any more queer food. The tummy won't stand it much longer," Teresa said in her tiny but determined voice.

"Well, my dear," I said, "I have no intention of coming all the way to France and eating in McDonald's. We could have stayed at home."

"Pity we didn't," said Seamus.

I wished he had too. Best to make the most of it. Only another thirteen days to go. Trouble with holidays is we bring not only our suitcases but our baggage too.

The evening meal went beautifully. I dined alone. Seafood tart to begin with, followed by vegetables in batter, deep-fried with a hot chilli sauce. And a bottle of the local rosé, pure nectar for a fraction the cost of a decent bottle at home.

A woman dining alone should always carry a file of papers to glance at and make notes. This protects from intrusion. The assumption is that she's a powerful businesswoman, straight from a Barbara Taylor Bradford novel with property and finance on her mind. Not someone who's been stood up or "on the make" as we used to say. Gentlemen hire companions at a dating agency to pretend they're desirable even when their belly reaches to their knees and their breath smells.

The others went either to McDonald's or the Café Anglais where they served suitably doctored French fare to fussy foreigners. This usually means there's no garlic and olive oil, the two things that make French cooking what it is.

When I swallowed the last delicious mouthful of lemon soufflé, I paid and walked towards the traffic-free Rue Masséna. A crowd had gathered around a man and a woman dressed as waiter and waitress pretending to be clockwork figures, each movement carefully planned and orchestrated, down to the last click when the music stopped and they shuddered to a halt.

I stayed to watch a second time when "Aren't they just wonderful" burst in on my eardrums. Sophia. Then recognition from her companion, Emily.

"It's Philippa. How did you get on on your own? Not a bother on you with all those Frenchmen around?"

"They're just like any other man. If you poke a finger in their eye, they go away. Otherwise, they just ignore you unless they hear you're filthy rich."

"My, aren't we cynical," Sophia said, head to one side like a parrot on a perch.

"A realist, Sophia."

"Let's see if we can find the others," Emily bustled along.

Waves and hallos brought us to Le Café International. Seamus was seated before a glass of his favourite black drink, looking like a little boy who has found a lost coin.

"Tinned," he confided. "But better than that h— p—."

The evening parade of the French on holiday was taking place. Up and down they went, stopping to chat here, a glass of pastis there. And all the time displaying their brown legs and firm bosoms as far up and down as decency or titillation would allow. Strange how women don't realise how anti-woman are the images created for them by men. There is something profoundly wrong with the desire on men's part to see women walk about semi-naked, a way of rendering them powerless. How can you take someone seriously when they've hardly anything on?

Little gurgles of delight issued from Seamus as a bosom flopped or a piece of knicker peeked out.

I turned to see if there was any escape when I spied Noreen in the gloom of the interior.

"Are you wishing to converse with yourself or with another?" I asked.

"For God's sake, sit down. Glad to see another human being. Them two give me the pip with their 'art' and their 'culture'. They're full of fancy words that are as empty as their heads."

Noreen sat back and folded her arms. "Emily has gone wafted altogether. She used to be a good laugh before that Sophia one appeared on the scene," she said, leaning towards me. "I was envying you having your decent supper in peace. Bags going with you next time. If there's one thing I'm doing when I've spent all this money getting here, it's sampling real French food."

"Good girl yourself. Why don't we split a good bottle of wine between us and make a start."

Dense cloud overshadowed the Baie des Anges and forced us to travel inland until the sun decided to return to Le Hot Spot. A tour of Gourdon, Les Gorges du Loup and Menton was arranged by Emily. Dickie and Percy decided not to come but to go instead to look for a particular kind of lavender soap Percy remembered as a boy. His mother used to bring it from her foreign trips with "friends".

"Lavender has a special meaning for me since. Gaye and I have a lavender hedge. Our bedroom is a beautiful mauvey-blue lavender and the quilt is the one Mummy left me, the palest of lavender blues."

That must be what did it for him. The mind boggles at the side effects of something as seemingly innocuous as a bar of soap layered with such deep, emotional meaning. A child will cling to anything in an insecure world. I didn't dare ask the shade of his underwear.

We left them at the hotel, Dickie flicking specks of dust from Percy's shoulders.

"He's a good sort," Gaye whispered to me, her eye on Percy. "Not a strong maleness about him but generous and considerate."

The bus was driven by one of those reckless French drivers who looked about sixteen. Of course we were forbidden to mount until the exact time the bus company dictated, even though common sense saw how ridiculous it was to keep us standing about. The French are great sticklers for rules and regulations. They find foreigners' contempt for them extremely irritating.

We wound round and round the mountains until we reached Gourdon and made a stop which had obviously been prearranged between the driver and the café owner. In return for our custom, he was presented with a huge plate of grilled steak and chips. I was more worried about the carafe of wine that disappeared with haste. Noreen shared my concern.

"Now we know why all those buses full of tourists crash all over the Continent," said Noreen.

We debated whether we'd be safer in the front, the back or the middle. We decided eventually on the front, beside the hammer encased in glass, to be broken in case of emergency.

Meanwhile, there was Gourdon to see, its touristy shops whose owners beckoned you in like sirens to the rocks. We smiled and passed on in crocodile to the Eagle's Nest where the inhabitants of the town used to flee and wait until the pirates from North Africa had finished looting and smashing their homes.

Up here, the air was cool, the hazy blue view stretching out to sea. Terraces of vines and vegetables in squares, rectangles and triangles spread like patchwork. The little town below perched on the rock, houses here and there clinging like limpets. On the downward pathway, an army of gardeners wrestled with columnar pines, planting them on the sloping ground with soil brought up in buckets. No space was allowed to be itself. All had to be prettified, to conform to some ill-conceived architectural plan. It was an aspect of French life I found stifling.

Only a handful of us made it to the top. Seamus and Gaye remained at the bottom, nursing beverages in tall glasses.

"Any more walking and I'll be laid up," Gaye laughed. Her ankles looked alarmingly swollen. Toxaemia and first babies came into my mind.

"Well, you'll have to take it easy. We have lunch in the Gorges du Loup, then a visit to Les Colombières, the most famous garden on the Riviera," I read the itinerary.

At the Gorges, the restaurant was built on wooden piles against the mountain. Sheer and without footholds.

Beside us, the river spiralled noisily down and disappeared from sight. Seamus got dizzy watching it and had to be pulled from the balcony by Noreen. The sun was out now, though our table was shaded by the cool green of a robinia.

I got some ice for Gaye and made her put her feet up.

"Don't fuss, Philippa. It's not an illness," she said, a little unkindly I felt.

"Not to be trifled with, all the same," I replied.

Seamus had his white face turned to the sun, contentment spread all over it for once.

"If this keeps up, we'll be able to go to the beach," he said, licking his lips.

It was Les Colombières that did it for Gaye. The bus was too hot for her to stay in it and she came with us, searching for the café the bus driver assured us was a mere stone's throw away. How to find it was another matter. The gardens were arranged in some sort of labyrinth of squares and open spaces with pieces of stonework on them. In one of these, hedged all round, we found a man sitting on a deck-chair doing some crochet work with blue wool.

"*Le café*, Monsieur?" I enquired.

He didn't bother to answer.

"Definitely French," I said, kicking the gravel noisily. "Only a Frenchman would dare to be that rude. Let's go to the left, they surely built the villa facing the sea."

Sure enough behind the ubiquitous colonnade of conifers was the proto-Roman villa of Les Colombières. A nasty-looking alsatian guarded its entrance. To the right, a faded wooden sign pointed to the café.

It had had its heyday. Rust vied with rot to destroy the remains of the tables and chairs. The cobbled yard was matted with dead grass.

The alsatian and its owner appeared behind the bar.

"*Citron pressé?*" I looked hopefully.

"*Non*," he said as he leaned across the rotting counter.

"*Jus de fruit? Orange peut-être?*"

"*Non.*"

"*Alors, eau minérale?*"

Water anyway. He produced two bottles and no glasses.

"This is the best we'll get. We really need some ice to get you cool."

"I must admit I'm feeling rotten. Even that awful bed in the hotel seems inviting. I wish Dunkie hadn't gone on. He's mad about gardens. Baby is moving about."

She rubbed her tummy, concern on her face. I daren't let her see mine. Enough was enough. I decided to order a taxi.

"Stay here, Gaye. Don't budge. I'll be back in five minutes."

In my most peremptory fashion, I ordered the bus-driver to call a taxi on his phone.

It arrived within minutes and for once the speed didn't bother me.

The bedroom was cool with the shutters drawn. I sprayed my bergamot and patchouli mixture everywhere to cool it some more and put a wet cloth on Gaye's forehead. She was soon asleep. I removed the damp cloth and sighed with relief onto the other bed. To lose a baby acquired with such difficulty would be tragic indeed.

Seamus got his wish. The following day began hot, airless and sunny, guaranteed to bring out the bronzed flesh of the Côte d'Azur.

Sure enough, by eight he had already gone, taking his breakfast roll, mirror sunglasses and hip flask with him for a day of breast-watching, like the old Algerian men sitting on the benches on the promenade.

Emily and Sophia decided it was the right time to visit Antibes, beloved of writers and artists. Percy and Dickie were still searching for lavender soap and "took a raincheck".

"I'll bring lunch," Sophia declared to us privileged

mortals. "Nothing too extraordinary – cheese, a baton, a piece of fruit."

"That will do fine, we don't want you to go to any trouble on holiday," I encouraged. "I'll bring the wine," I said, with emphasis.

I collected the empty five-litre water container from Gaye's room and brought it to the co-op where I queued with the ordinary folk of the old town. The wine flowed like syrup from the brass tap, pumped up from some vast tank in the cool basement. Cheaper than buying it by the bottle. However, lugging five litres of wine across Nice is no joke. The men would have to go next time.

I left a strawberry tart and some fresh water with Gaye before I left.

"You know, Philippa," she said, "people can say what they like about you. For my money you're worth the whole lot of them put together. I really appreciate how thoughtful and kind you are."

I was torn between being angry that anyone should have the cheek to criticise me and being touched at her appreciation. I simply said goodbye.

Sophia was arrayed in her summer gear. Yellow Bermudas contrasting with Tan-in-a-Tube legs and cream silk top over underwired bra to give some sort of shape. The broad red hairband hid a multitude and protected the peroxide at the same time. A clever woman, everything figured out to the last, even the varnished toe-nails. Like being able to work out the age of a tree by its rings, it was now impossible to count those telling ridges on the toes and give the game away.

Emily was restrained in blue and white to the knee and a straw hat. Noreen threw caution to the wind and wore her tank top, contour-hugging her C-cup roundness, and matching trousers. As for myself, well, I dressed as if for the jungle in shorts and safari blouse, white, of course, to hide the patches of perspiration. Robert Dahling, who had been noticeable by his absence for the past few days, descended the stairs in glorious technicolour. Palm leaves and bright yellow fruits climbed all over him, except for the arms and below the knees where the hair fell in spidery hanks. I hate it when men actually look as if they've just come down from the trees. The least they can do is a bleach job like the rest of us.

Sophia and Emily walked ahead to the station, tête-à-tête, leaving me to Dahling's mercies.

"You've been hiding yourself while the rest of us have been getting blisters sight-seeing," I said, attempting civility.

"The old bread-basket, you know," he said, tapping his midriff. "Change of scene and all that."

"'Staying close to the porcelain', the French call it," I lied and didn't dare look at his face. He sensibly said nothing.

Feeling slightly guilty, I went on, "You didn't miss much, so far. *Plus ça change* . . . "

"Never could understand the lingo. Latin scholar, all right, a bit of German . . . "

"It means that no matter how much things seem to change, they end up the same. Like a change of government."

"Running round in circles theory. Very interesting."

I was bored already.

Tiny dogs on leads were being given their morning walk, to soil the pavements. The reason the French walk with their head bent. Nothing worse than the stink of a poo when the dog has been fed on tinned food. I noticed Dahling had already collided with one and was busy trying to leave the sticky mess behind.

"You'll need an acid bath to get rid of it, I'm afraid," I informed him. He didn't seem particularly grateful.

Fortunately the train was full with only single seats available, so we scattered and I had my thoughts to myself. No doubt the best place for them. I was already missing Gerald. He likes my sense of humour.

The train was full of tourists trying to read the names of the stations, discovering it was their stop just as the train was about to take off again and getting stuck in the automatic doors with suitcases and haversacks.

A cool breeze blew in from the shore as we walked the hefty step from the station to the little fortified town of Antibes. The market was in progress up the steps, at Place Masséna. Emily and Sophia handled the fruits, smelling and feeling them. Dahling stood a respectful distance, hands on his hips. I smiled at him for no particular reason. A mistake. He took it as an invitation.

"Shall we go and have some coffee while the two housewives select some delicacies?"

How could I refuse?

We wandered down the steps at the far side of the market and along the narrow street lined with cafés. I sat beneath an umbrella and let Dahling penetrate the interior.

A tall, blond man with Steve McQueen eyes and skimpy, white shorts came and wiped the table. He was followed by an even taller blond man with black top and shorts who placed a hand, *en passant*, on his bottom. We had picked the place where "the lads" hung out.

Dahling came out carrying the coffees, looking furtive.

"Guess who's in there?"

"Graham Greene – no, he died last year. Let me see . . . "

He waved a hand impatiently. "Dickie and Percy."

"I didn't realise Antibes was famous for its lavender soap. No need for us to look so guilty, all the same," I said, taking a cup of creamy coffee from the tray.

"Even you must admit it's a bit embarrassing. They have wives, don't they?"

"Marriage is no cure, Robert."

He looked at me over his cup with the same puzzled expression as Teresa and Dotty do at times.

"So here you are!" Sophia and Emily, breathless with bags of fruit, looked at us crossly.

"We were buying this stuff for you. We could have done with some help."

"You know I can't stand fruit, Emily. Your effort was in vain for me," I protested.

"And my little bread-basket wouldn't take the strain, I'm afraid," Dahling said.

"Really Robert, you and that stomach of yours. You let it run your life," Sophia screeched, the sun getting to her.

"Thank you very much for the coffee, Robert," I said, gathering my things to make haste.

"So, it's to be Robert this and Robert that, is it? Well, I've had more than enough of you and 'Philippa says' and 'Philippa makes such good ones' not to mention 'Ask Philippa'. Ask you? I wouldn't ask you the time of day. You're the sort of person who takes over, who ingratiates themselves into people's affections in order to run their lives for them!"

A small audience was gathering. The lads were lapping it up, copy for their next tiff.

As coolly as possible, I said, "You can rest assured, Sophia, that you are most welcome to your life. There is enough misery in the world without me having to go looking for it."

She boo-hooed at this and collapsed onto a chair. The two lads were buzzing round her at once, bringing coffee, offering croissants, or perhaps a little chocolate cake?

She wept into every morsel. Robert hung his head in shame. Emily held her hand, whispering consolations. I felt as if I was somehow responsible, when all I did was defend myself. People always rush to the one with the tears. I shed mine in private.

Bewildered, I wandered off towards the little back streets, between houses with wrought-iron balconies and window boxes of exquisite flowers. One of these streets led to a small park. I sat on a bench and watched a group of men play pétanque, their musical tones exploding now and again as someone scored. Tiny, dark children were playing at a fountain, their mothers chatting and knitting at the same time. A baby cried and its mother cooed.

I pulled out a postcard of the Baie des Anges and wrote:

Dear Gerald,

Miss you terribly. Like a drowning person, I keep seeing my life unravel before me. Next week we go to Aix. Don't expect it will be any better.

Love, P.

A bit strong, perhaps. But it was exactly how I felt. As evening began to fall, I wandered towards the beach. It was dog-walking time again. Beribboned poodles yapped and skipped about like clockwork toys. In the distance, at the end of a wooden jetty that, in summer, would be crammed with naked bodies, two familiar figures, arms around each other, faces locked in a kiss, were silhouetted against the pink sky. Dickie and Percy. Love comes in the strangest of forms but it's love just the same. Who's to dictate where we should find our happiness? Though I felt for Emily, where did she fit into all this? Gaye Greene was certainly cared for by Percy and the baby looked forward to. But Emily? I suppose she had the dubious consolation of children.

Tired and thoroughly fed up, I sat in the bar that evening and watched Seamus, fresh from the fleshpots of the Côte d'Azur, order a stiff drink.

"Well, Seamus," I ventured. "Are we really all the same skin deep?"

He stopped to wipe the sweat that tricked like tears down his face.

"Seen better at home," he whispered and swallowed his drink. "I think it's past me bedtime," he winked and padded out of the lounge and up the stairs.

Poor Noreen. Only one thing worse than having no sex would be have Seamus breathe hotly all over you.

I tried not to count the days till I returned home but I was pleased we were into our second week and bound for Aix. Two things I like about the town, the Café des Deux Garcons and the *calissons*; diamond shapes of iced marzipan. I made straight for the Provençal shop and bought several lengths of brightly patterned fabric to be made into curtains and chair coverings.

Unfortunately, for some reason I couldn't fathom, the Archaeological Society had developed a split. Noreen, Gaye and I appeared to be on one side and Emily, Sophia, Teresa and Dotty on the other. The men seemed to sit dumb and say nothing, except for Robert who chatted to me when Sophia wasn't looking. Though Clara had joined us with Mo, we hardly ever saw them. They were busy "resting", Clara said. Probably one on top of the other, though I didn't enquire. In the mornings, Clara bore all the marks of love's war with weeping beard rash and a necklace of lovebites. The vision of mating they conjured up was enough to put one off sex for life.

Dunkie was lost to us. Found a lithe, brown-eyed beauty on the beach at Menton where he had decided to stay a while. Gaye wasn't the least bit put out.

"He needs to be free," she said. "It's worked out rather well."

Like a chosen drone, outlived his use.

The split is healed to pay a visit to the Camargue. The more there are, the less the bus costs.

"Just like the Bog of Allen," Seamus said.

He's right, except that the air is warmer and there are flamingoes.

"Look at the little black cattle, just like Philippa's," I heard from the back. As usual Noreen and I were at the front, beside the hammer.

Reminders of home brought a pall of sadness. What was I doing here, among these people when I could be at home? It seemed to be a recurring pattern. Was I running from or to something? Perhaps loneliness was the bugbear, the need for some semblance of human contact – but this brought merely pain and misery. Unable to answer such mind-bending questions, I snoozed my way through the Camargue to Avignon.

"This is where we'll see the 'Tarasque'." Emily bent forward from the seat behind. "The queer sculpture of a monster with a head between its paws," she said to my barely awake look.

"Sounds a bit like life. We're all in the grip of some imagined monster or another," I said.

Sure enough, when we got to the Lapidary Museum the sight of the thing gave us all a shock.

"To think it was made by the Celts, our ancestors," Noreen said, horrified.

"Doesn't surprise me one bit," said Emily. "They went in for as much decapitation as we indulge in nowadays. One day it's one person's head on the metaphorical plate, tomorrow another. We're great at pointing the finger," Emily concluded with surprising insight.

"With justification," Sophia butted in where she was not wanted. "We have a duty to expose any wrongs and injustice."

"It's a decision most of us are ill-fit to make," I said in my most scathing tone. I watched with disgust as Robert Dahling put a restraining hand on dear little Sophia's arm.

"Sure maybe he's just giving it a bit of a talking-to,"

Seamus said, staring at the statue, sucking his lips in and out.

Death seemed to be everywhere. Our next port of call was the cemetery of Ste Véran where John Stuart Mill and his wife, Harriet, languish. Just the thing to help one get away from it all. The grave slab was interesting, full of effusive praise for Harriet and the tiniest of spaces for John Stuart's name.

"Imagine he was so upset at her death, he had a house built overlooking the cemetery," Teresa made the longest speech I had yet heard. Impressed by devotion. Every woman's dream, when all men really want is sex and food and not necessarily in that order.

"He couldn't let go of her," Noreen said, smiling seductively at Seamus.

I stared at the slab. Had I let go of Jack? Did I forgive myself for his death? There are only the questions. We find the answers when we no longer need to know them.

Thoroughly depressed, we decided to split up and meet back at the bus. I decided to search for the bridge where people "danced in a ring". No one else seemed interested, preferring the comfort of a carafe of wine to dispel the ghosts.

Leaving the walled town by the Porte de la Ligne, I walked towards the swelling waters of the Rhône. Sitting on its grassy banks I looked west where only half the Pont Saint-Bénézet hung across the river, leading nowhere, the thousands who danced and sang beneath it now blown into the wind.

On the far bank, behind a long stretch of wire fencing was the check shirt of Robert, gold sunglasses glinting. Catching sight of me he stopped and grabbed at the fence, like a monkey at the bars of a cage. I had an almost overwhelming urge to swim across the river and join him but I restrained myself. The frightening truth was that, at that moment, he seemed the most desirable person in the world.

The journey back to Aix seemed endless and in spite of the sunshine and colour, without comfort. There is an ache that the sun augments. I thought of Gerald. Gaye slept most of the way, her bump encased in her arms, bobbing up and down. Emily and Sophia seemed quieter. Robert sat opposite, staring out the window, looking miserable. At least he doesn't pretend. Teresa and Dotty continued their endless whispering at the back of the bus. Perhaps they were reciting passages of The Rubáiyát to each other when all along we thought they were chatting.

I made for my room as quickly as possible, took every stitch off, wrapped myself in a towel and made for the showers. I let the glorious water beat on my skin for an eternity. There's such comfort in just feeling. It's when we think about feeling that the trouble starts. I tied my long wet hair into a towel, dried myself off and felt able for anything. Except perhaps the Archaeological Society.

In the dim corridor a shadow hovered, silhouetted against the window at the bottom. A split second's disbelief as the outline matched known shapes in my mind.

"Gerald? Is that you?"

No reply. For a horrible second I thought I'd made a giant fool of myself.

He came towards me, beige shirt and trousers to match.

"You could have said! You gave me a helluva fright. What on earth are you doing here? How did you know where to find me? Is there something wrong? Why aren't you talking?"

And then I saw the softness in his eyes, his arms reaching for me. Trust me to yapper on when all that was needed was 'hello'.

In that dim comfortless corridor we hugged and hugged. I felt I was home, this was it, this should last forever.

"Better let you dry your hair," he said, taking my key and opening the door. "'Wet hair equals chill' mother always said."

"That was in the cold north, not in the sunny South of France. Besides, where is she now?"

He laughed. "Died of pneumonia! But if she hadn't gone to church on that wet November morning six months previously, none of it would have happened, she kept repeating at the end."

I untied the towel on my head and let my hair float out the window to dry. Gerald sat on the bed.

"It was nice to get your card, to know it was me you shared your difficulties with."

"I'll have to stop sending you cards if you come to rescue me every time."

"Isn't that what friends are for?"

I was touched by his answer but felt too choked to reply. He got up from the bed and came towards me. Frightened to let him see my face, I turned towards the evening sun.

His hand touched my shoulder. I began to weep uncontrollably.

"It's okay," he said gently, "it's okay."

"Must be all this sun, not able for it."

"Now don't make a joke of it. It sounds to me like it goes a lot deeper than that."

He was right, of course. How deep I didn't dare contemplate.

We managed to give everyone the slip and went towards the Cours Mirabeau and turned left at the fountain.

"You seem to know your way around here," I accused rather than asked.

"Surely the Cours Mirabeau is part of everyone's education?" Gerald winked and steered me into a tiny restaurant where a group of musicians were arranging themselves in a corner with much noise, chatter and swallowing of wine.

"This is our hors d'oeuvre, *Crêpe à la Provençale*. We'll have our main course down the street, first left."

"I'm yours to command, Gerald."

"A likely story!"

In the tiny *crêperie*, we sat and listened to the best of Bessie Smith in English pronounced *à la française*, while a beautiful North African girl in a long white beaded dress served us cider in pottery goblets and cooked our crêpes on a cast-iron slab in the middle of the room. The music, the cider, the heat of an Aix evening combined to recreate the uncontrollable sadness I felt earlier. Now was no time to cry. But once given a signal, once given even a shred of existence, the floodgates open. My napkin was soggy within minutes. I thought Gerald was too busy with the music to notice. But no.

"That feeling again?" he asked.

I nodded.

"Here, have a decent hankie." He handed me a freshly pressed linen handkerchief smelling of freesia. It was all I needed. My crêpe lay on my plate, getting soggier by the minute.

"I was thinking. Someone I used to know."

"You must have liked him very much."

"The worst of it is, I never knew how much until I lost him."

"What a terrible burden to bear."

"Since coming here, all sorts of ghosts have risen together. You see, it's where we lived and . . ."

"Loved?"

"Yes. Yes . . ." I blew my nose. "It's strange, Gerald. I've been so busy feeling sorry for myself, feeling guilty for Jack's death that I've forgotten about the happy times. I think that's why, in Aran, when I, you know . . . jumped up, it was to do with being close to someone and the fear that I might lose them."

"I understand. Very sensible of you to do that. I remember being cross with myself for being so cheeky."

"You could never be that even if you tried."

"Well, I'd like to be a little cheeky just now." He shifted a bit in his chair. I became alarmed when he took my hand.

"Philippa," he said softly. "I've become very . . . "

"Thought we'd never find you! I've been in every café in the place. There's been a phone call." Emily shattered into the present.

Gerald pulled out a seat.

"Oh! It's you," she said to Gerald while giving me an accusing look.

I looked over her shoulder to see whether she had a follower.

"We all split up to find you and agreed to meet at that fancy café in the main street. Sophia is behaving really badly and refused to come, even when I told her it was urgent."

"Is there a problem?" Gerald asked the question I didn't dare.

"Well, your brother Andy phoned the main building," Emily began breathlessly. "And they came up with the message. Sophia's been boasting about how good her French is but when push came to shove she hadn't a clue what they were saying. And then she'd the cheek to blame the Midi accent."

Trouble in Paradise.

"So between Gaye and myself and our school French, we managed to work it all out. The gist of it is, Andy's got engaged and wanted you to be the first to know!"

Terrific.

"Did he mention who the . . . lucky woman was?"

"Yes. A kind of church name. It's on the tip of my tongue."

It had to be Gloria. Hard at it as soon as my back was turned.

Gerald offered a glass of cider but Emily refused.

"No thanks. Dickie and I have arranged a meal together, just the two of us. We've a lot to talk about."

She looked miserable at the prospect and went off with considerably less energy than she came.

I ordered more cider.

"By the way," Gerald said, lifting the beaker to his beautiful mouth. "It was Andy who told me where you were staying. I phoned when I got your card. He seemed very pleased with himself. Only said 'Fair dinkum' once. I gather his news doesn't please you?"

Marry a tree-killer and you could end up a stump.

"A chainsaw-happy pig-killer was not the person I would have wished for a sister-in-law."

He looked at me to see if I was joking. I didn't move a muscle.

"Now, where were we before being rudely interrupted?"

I had too much pride to tell him.

"Yes, I remember now. I was telling you how very interested I was becoming in farming. You mentioned something about free-range chickens."

I could have sworn that wasn't where we'd left off, but I said nothing.

"How about advising me on what to do with the old ancestral? Big sister wants me to keep a beady eye on the old man. Perhaps he would like some company for a while."

The soggy crêpe was taking massive amounts of concentration.

"It's a rather nice house. I think you'll like it. Bit of a turrety-thing round the back which Father turned into a library."

"Really?" I said between mouthfuls. I had my goblet replenished.

"Yes. Full of farming books going back to the year dot. There's a piece of woodland, about ten or so acres . . . "

"A . . . small wood."

He swallowed his cider and asked for a refill. The lady in flowing white smiled at him.

"Of course, there are another several hundred – for goodness sake, Philippa! I'll get cross with all this nonsense. Can't you see what I'm about?"

I could see it was some sort of variation on the "do you want to be buried with my people?" routine but I was too well brought up to be forward.

"You're inviting me to visit, Gerald. Am I right?"

He swallowed the cider as if it were water.

"Well, a sort of extended visit . . . "

"I see."

"For God's sake, Philippa, will you marry me?"

"Yes."